PETER
PUMPKIN
GOES
to
SCHOOL

PETER PUMPKIN GOES to SCHOOL

Peter Nanra

ARCHWAY
PUBLISHING

Archway Publishing books may be ordered through booksellers or by contacting:

Archway Publishing
1663 Liberty Drive
Bloomington, IN 47403
www.archwaypublishing.com
1 (888) 242-5904

ISBN: 978-1-4808-4184-0 (sc)
ISBN: 978-1-4808-4197-0 (hc)
ISBN: 978-1-4808-4198-7 (e)

Library of Congress Control Number: 2016921393

Print information available on the last page.

Archway Publishing rev. date: 12/23/2016

CHAPTER 1
FIRST DAY

I awoke to the sound of, "Ouch!" This was not the first time. It seemed like a daily occurrence. The sound had almost become my own personal alarm bell. Sometimes it was annoying, but for the most part, I just accepted it as my morning wake-up call. The scream was from my brother. He had stubbed his toe against the side of my bed.

I opened my eyes and yawned. I watched while he hopped around our house, with both his hands wrapped around his right foot, trying desperately not to fall. After a few bounces, he did just that, landing on my bed, near my feet. I saw tears form in his eyes. I was sure he was hoping the pain would subside. I thought he would be lucky if his toe wasn't broken again. It was probably starting to turn red. He did break two bones in there last year. Dr. Pumpkin fit him with a walking boot, and he had to use crutches for a week. I would hate for that to happen to me. My pumpkin skin and bones are too soft and vulnerable to survive a smash like that. I try to take every precaution I can to preserve my body. My orange skin can bruise quite quickly, even at the slightest physical contact with any object. My head and body are bigger than the average five-year-old female pumpkin. My stem is wider, and my eyes bulge more than they should. I know it.

We all agreed that my bed was too close to our front door, but we lived in such a cramped house that our options of moving it away were limited. And besides, it was his own fault. He knew his quickest path to the front door was to pass by my bed. He should be more careful.

"I can't believe I just did that again," he moaned to himself.

I continued watching as he slowly calmed himself. He took a heavy breath, got up, collected his school bag, and raced out the front door. This time he did not run into any obstacles. He was headed for school, no doubt.

My goodness. School. How could I have forgotten? Today was the first day of school.

I threw the bed covers off of me, got out of bed, and hurried myself into the bathroom. I washed my face and cleaned my teeth. There was no time for my morning bubble bath today. I wondered if I was late. I tied a purple bow on my stem. I started looking around the house for my school bag. I checked on my bedside table and then underneath my bed. But wait a minute. Did I even have a school bag? No, I didn't. I got so confused sometimes. I must have been nervous.

I left the house and made sure I closed the door behind me. I hoped I didn't have to bring a school bag. I didn't recall anyone telling me to bring one. I hoped I wasn't late. I didn't think it was good karma to be late on the first day of school. Oh well. Nothing I could do about it now. There was no sense in stressing over it. Still, I found myself walking quickly north on column TY07, which then merged into column CD03. I was almost running. I noticed there were hardly any pumpkins outside. *I must be late*, I thought. *Everyone must be at school.*

As I entered the eye through the west gate, I saw Mr. Pumpkin bending down to pick up his cane. He was very old. He lived next door, to the north. He must have dropped it. I had to stop and help him.

"Hello, Mr. Pumpkin. Here, let me help," I offered.

"Oh, thank you so much, dear. I need all the help I can get. Shouldn't you be in school?" he asked.

"Yes. I'm just on my way now. Which way are you walking? We can walk together if you want. You can keep me company on the way. Here, you can hold my arm."

I picked up his cane and held it in my right hand while he grabbed my left arm. We walked slowly through the rose garden. That's when Ms. Pumpkin shouted my name from a near distance, and walked toward us. She had been in the soil of the rose garden, digging or planting or something. I didn't know. The gardeners did such a great job of keeping our patch smelling clean and fresh. They ensured our patch remained beautiful, lush, and green and full of fancy flowers. It was too bad that fall was approaching and most of these flowers would disappear soon.

Ms. Pumpkin wanted me to hurry to school. She seemed annoyed with me. She told me to leave Mr. Pumpkin where he was standing, so I pulled away. But maybe that was not such a good idea because he wanted my left arm to hold onto while he maintained his balance. But since I left him without any warning, he stumbled and fell to the ground—almost right on his face, too. That looked ugly.

"My goodness. Are you okay?" I had to ask.

By this time, Ms. Pumpkin had arrived and said she would help. It was probably a good idea that she took over. I hoped the old pumpkin would be okay. I was sure he would be.

I continued on my route through the rose garden by myself, heading westward. Then the rose garden turned into the tulip garden. This route took me over twenty minutes to travel from my house to the school. I lived on the east side, while the school was located on the west side of the patch. I turned south when I reached Star River and walked over the Water Gate Bridge to cross the river. And up ahead there was plenty of green grass and open space. Another twenty-minute walk or so from here would take me to the greenhouse and farm. The golf course separated the greenhouse from the school. There were two soccer fields behind the school that bordered the tall trees that separated the patch from the city of Burrowsville.

Our school was a three-story, old brick building. It was built many years ago by some of the original pumpkins who lived in this patch. Upgrades had been done to the school over the years. A wooden extension was built a few years ago. As I opened the main door, which was very heavy, I started to get even more nervous—a little antsy feeling inside my stomach. It was going to be weird seeing my friends in an educational-type setting. Inside the building, there were many hallways and numerous classrooms. I would be on the main level, in hallway number four, toward the back. I was quite sure of it. The halls were quiet. Everyone must be in class, I thought. *Even the teachers.* When I arrived at hallway number four, I started looking at the posted class lists as I slowly walked past each room. When I had reached near the end of the hall, I had to stop. These must have been the classrooms for the five-year-old pumpkins. We were split up between three different classrooms. I had to verify that I was indeed in class 1, as I had previously been told.

Class 1: Ms. Perlina Pumpkin

Palmer Pumpkin
Pannette Pumpkin
Pashelle Pumpkin

Pebbles Pumpkin
Peter Pumpkin
Petrina Pumpkin
Picasso Pumpkin
Pippi Pumpkin
Plato Pumpkin
Polo Pumpkin
Pom Pom Pumpkin

Good. I was with my friends, as I had been told last night. And it was good we were assigned Ms. Pumpkin as our teacher. I had been told she was the nicest of the three teachers. But wait. I didn't see Pavneet listed. Which class was she in? What had happened? Why wasn't she in our class? We had been told that she was going to be in our class. We had many meetings with the elders to sort this out. And I thought we had. Oh, that's so bad. So unfortunate. I scanned the other class lists to see where she was assigned.

Class 2: Mr. Pius Pumpkin

Pandora Pumpkin
Pandria Pumpkin
Patience Pumpkin
Peanut Pumpkin
Pecan Pumpkin
Pekka Pumpkin
Penny Pumpkin
Pepper Pumpkin
Pickle Pumpkin
Porter Pumpkin
Prudence Pumpkin

She was not assigned to Class 2.

Class 3: Ms. Pearl Pumpkin

Panic Pumpkin
Pavneet Pumpkin
Perses Pumpkin
Ping Pumpkin
Pippa Pumpkin
Plunder Pumpkin
Pluto Pumpkin
Pong Pumpkin
Prima Pumpkin
Prime Pumpkin
Primo Pumpkin

There she was, listed in class 3. How had she ended up in class 3? Okay. Never mind. I couldn't be worried about that now.

I was so nervous when I opened the classroom door. Inside, all I heard was silence. Everyone was staring at me. Why? Just because I was late? My goodness. What was the big deal? *Everyone should just relax and not be so judgmental*, I thought. And then I had to locate an empty desk. I was starting to get all sweaty. My face was warm, and my body felt achy. That had been a long walk for me. I needed to catch my breath and regain my composure. I had to deal with finding a seat with all the eyes focused on me. Talk about pressure.

"Sit next to Peter. Quickly," Ms. Pumpkin said, breaking the silence. She seemed annoyed with me.

I sat down next to Peter in the seat that had my name on a banner draped all over the desk. I hadn't noticed the banner when I had entered the room. On the way down the aisle, I stepped on someone's foot. That was the second "ouch" I heard that day. I heard a few students giggle due to that incident. Peter gave me a comforting smile. I wondered whose foot I had just stepped on. I was so nervous that I wasn't even sure if I smiled back at Peter. Once I took my seat, I scanned the room. I hung out with my friends all the time, but it still seemed weird sitting in class like this with them. A million thoughts were going through my head.

"Pannette," I heard Ms. Pumpkin say. I think she wanted to take attendance. Good. Then maybe I wasn't so late.

"Pannette," she said again. I wondered why.

The room was all quiet. Everyone was now focused on her and away from me.

"Pannette!" she said a third time. This time she seemed upset. I could tell by the sharp tone in her voice. "We need to get started."

What? What did she want? Was I supposed to say something? She knew I was there.

"Yes, Ms. Pumpkin. I'm here," I finally replied.

"Thank you," she said in a sarcastic tone.

Yes. That's me. My name is Pannette Pumpkin.

CHAPTER 2
ROLL CALL

Was it really necessary for me to say anything? Was she waiting for me this whole time, so she could take attendance? She could have called on someone else. *Why am I always first? Just because my name comes first alphabetically, it shouldn't mean I get called on first. It seems kind of silly. I think school is silly. Actually, no. Wait. Palmer would have been called first.*

"Why were you late this morning?" she asked. She started writing in her notebook. I didn't think she was going to let this go.

"I forgot." It was the only thing I could think of to say.

"How could you forget about coming to school?" she responded.

What? What kind of a question was that? Was that supposed to be a question? Well if I realized I forgot, then I wouldn't have forgotten in the first place. I mean, how could I know to forget something? If I knew to forget something, then I wouldn't have forgotten. I didn't know how to respond, so I didn't say anything. I just shrugged my shoulders, hoping she would continue on with the roll call.

She spent a considerable amount of time writing notes in her book—about me, I was sure. We all waited for her. Then she called out, "Pashelle Pumpkin."

"I'm here, Ms. Pumpkin," she replied.

I must admit, I did feel a little silly arriving late. Everyone was staring at me there for a while. I should have set my alarm clock last night, but I forgot. And don't ask me how I forgot.

Pashelle was a very close friend of mine. We hung out a lot. She came over to my house often. She could be kind of bossy sometimes, especially when she got impatient. Many times when we were all bored and didn't know what to do, she would go and do something, expecting us to follow her. She would do it out of the blue, sometimes without consulting any of us. And we had no choice but to follow and join her. She liked to keep busy and stay active. She always seemed to have something on the agenda—always something on the go. She loved to visit the city, where people lived. She was always submitting our names for field trips to the city whenever there was a chance. Now that we were in school full time, I was sure she was going to keep herself, and us, even busier.

When Ms. Pumpkin finished writing her notes about Pashelle, she called, "Pebbles Pumpkin."

I didn't know Pebbles very well, so I could not really tell you anything about her. I did see her a lot though. I saw her in the lounge all the time, but we had never really had a conversation with each other. We hadn't done anything together. She seemed super nice though.

After a long wait, she called out, "Peter."

Peter said hello and waved to the teacher.

I was sitting next to Peter. I thought, *Oh, how great. Terrific. I have to sit next to him. I mean, he can be quite a bore sometimes. Maybe we will all change seats sometime during the school year—mix things up a bit. I might suggest that to Ms. Pumpkin.*

He was to my right. There was no desk to my left. I was seated in the middle column of the third row of seats. There were six rows in total in this classroom. Each row had three seats, except this row. I wasn't sure why they didn't put a desk next to me. There was a closet there. Maybe they thought that whoever needed to open the closet would need the space to use it too.

Up ahead, behind Ms. Pumpkin's desk, was a shelf full of books. There were four shelves, all full of books.

All the desks had a cubbyhole to store items. It was kind of like an underground parking lot like we see on television. Well no, not really. Well, kind of.

And there were no windows in there—none, not to look outside or even to let some light in. I thought it was going to be a damp and dreary winter.

I turned to look at Peter. He saved Pavneet last year. Pavneet was taken by witches during trick or treating. Or were they ghosts? They just grabbed her and took off to a forest. And Peter chased them. He rescued her. That whole incident was scary. We all thought that Pavneet was going to be permanently missing or dead. She was tied to a tree, and she was going to be eaten alive. But Peter brought her back home safe and sound. I spent the whole night in the hospital with her afterward. She was sick from rat poison too. That whole situation was ugly. I helped her feel comfortable when she spent the night in the hospital. I eased her pain. That's what Ms. Pumpkin said. I brought her water and food, like a nurse would do. We talked all night. I read to her to help her fall asleep. Actually, I think I fell asleep before her. I was so tired after trick or treating that evening.

I wondered why Pavneet was not in our class. I asked Peter.

"Quiet please," Ms. Pumpkin interrupted. Like, weren't we allowed to say anything during roll call?

We watched her while she wrote her notes about Peter. I wondered what she could have possibly written. I wondered what she wrote about me. She probably wrote that I was very helpful. I was. Everyone knew it.

"Petrina Pumpkin."

Petrina was such a diva. She thought the whole world revolved around her. She thought she was so popular. And in a way, she was. She thought everyone liked her. But trust me when I say that everyone did not like her. The only reason she was so popular was because she was Peter's sister. I mean, everyone knew Peter. And Petrina loved the attention. She often referred to me as her best friend, but I was not sure she was my best friend. Don't get me wrong—I liked her. But I had lots of other friends too. She liked to come over to my house, and we hung out all the time. I probably had told her everything about myself. She knew me like a book, and I knew everything about her too.

I turned around and said hello to Pippi. She smiled back at me. I smiled at the pumpkins up ahead too, when they turned their heads around. I managed to whisper a hello to Petrina. We were instructed to look straight ahead and focus on the bookshelves. Ms. Pumpkin didn't want any disruption.

Petrina was sitting in the front row, to the right. She was right near the door. That might get annoying for her after a while. I mean, who likes sitting near a public door, watching it open and close all day long with that squeaky sound? Next to her was Palmer, and then Polo was to the far left.

In the second row, from left to right were Pebbles, Pashelle, and Pom Pom.

And behind us were Pippi, Plato, and Picasso.

The last two rows at the back were empty.

"Picasso Pumpkin."

Picasso was a really good drawer. And he liked to paint and sculpt. He was a very talented artist. He attempted many of these types of artistic endeavors. He painted a beautiful picture of space and the stars and gave it to Petrina. I asked him to draw a picture for me too. I needed to talk to him about that. He expressed his feelings through his work, I thought. He was playfully shy—quite reserved and quiet. Sometimes he drew funny and weird pictures of pumpkins, and people, to make fun of them, especially famous people.

What in the world could Ms. Pumpkin be writing down? So much information on each pumpkin.

My life was going to be different now. My friends used to come over to my house in the afternoons. But now, we'd all be at school. School can be a life-altering experience.

Ms. Pumpkin continued on with attendance. "Pippi Pumpkin," she called.

I didn't know Pippi that well either. The only thing I could tell you about her was that she liked to wear these really long stockings that went all the way up past her knees. She had some pairs of stockings that went all the way up to her waist. I had never seen her when she wasn't wearing her stockings.

"Plato Pumpkin."

Plato was smart—super-smart and extremely bright. He had to be the smartest pumpkin in our class. And it seemed that each year, it was getting more difficult to understand him. A few years back, I could. But now when he tried to explain something, I almost needed someone to translate what he said.

We are told that pumpkins are sharper and quicker than people at an early age, because we mature faster. It was obvious. We could tell. We didn't need to be told this. Sometimes we met four-, five-, and six-year-old children when they visited our patch, and they had difficulty following our conversation and understanding what we said. It was almost like we had a better understanding of English than they did, that our brains functioned faster and quicker. Pumpkins could learn and understand concepts and ideas much more clearly. But Plato seemed really advanced for our age. Ms. Pumpkin spent a long time writing notes about Plato.

When was breakfast? Weren't we going to have breakfast? I was starting to get hungry. Didn't we get a break? School was different from preschool, we were told. We know, anyway. Last year, we were in preschool. We only came to the school for two hours and not even every day. But now, we spent eight hours here at the school, and every day. Well, not weekends. Roll call was starting to get boring. And we weren't even allowed to say anything while she was taking her notes. I wondered if we would be allowed to read these notes.

"Polo Pumpkin," she called after a lengthy delay.

Polo liked sports. He had told me many times that he would like to ride on a horse—strange request for a pumpkin. Polo was very muscular. He had very broad shoulders. He looked tough, like he'd been in multiple fights. There were some scars on his face. He looked very rugged. He would do really well as a security guard. Polo was one of my closest friends. And Plato. And Pavneet. Pashelle. Petrina. Well, I had lots of friends, but those were the pumpkins I hung out with, mostly. And I had two brothers, Patrick and Parson. They were both one year older than I.

"Pom Pom Pumpkin." I think she was the last one on the list. Or maybe not. I cannot remember.

Actually her given name at birth was Pom, but she had more trouble understanding English at an early age. So many times we had to repeat her name. We had to say Pom two times. We all thought she was deaf. But really she was fine. She was a little slow, but she had no hearing problems. So we said Pom two times, and the name just stuck on her. She had grown up knowing her name was Pom Pom.

Her older brother, Pompeo, had the elected elders officially change her name last year.

After she completed writing her notes on Pom Pom, Ms. Pumpkin said it was time for a break. My goodness. Finally. I think she could have written a complete book with all the notes she compiled. Pashelle bolted from her seat and ran out the door. I noticed she was getting restless and impatient. She had spent the last hour bobbing and twisting in her seat. She was the first one out the door. At first I thought she just wanted to beat Polo to the door. But we found out later she had to use the toilet. It was anticlimactic.

"Can't you be on time for the first day of school? Why were you late?" asked Petrina. We went out the door at the end of the hallway. We were facing west. We were at the back of the school, where the soccer fields are visible. There was a playground as well, up ahead to the right. And there were lots of benches.

"Oh, I'm so mad. I'm sitting next to Palmer. Ms. Pumpkin did this on purpose. Who draws up the seating plan? I bet Ms. Pumpkin told her about that incident last year. That trust experiment." She was ranting. I had to change the subject.

"Just wait. Hold on!" I barked in a stern voice. "Just drop it, okay? There's nothing wrong him. Learn to be nice to everyone."

"What do you mean? I am nice to everyone. I'm the most social pumpkin I know."

"C'mon. Let's see if we can find Pavneet. I thought she was going to be in our class. Isn't that what Mr. Pumpkin said? I mean, we had all those meetings, pleading our case."

"What meetings? I didn't attend any meetings. What are you talking about?"

"We had all those meetings with the elders."

"We talked to Mr. Pumpkin two times—one time to ask for

Pavneet to be moved to our class, and another for him to say he would think about it."

"We had at least three meetings. Four," I countered.

"Hey." Polo and Plato had just joined us, and there came Pashelle. And there was Pavneet. "It's Pavneet. Over there. I think she saw us. I think she's coming over here."

"Yeah. I think so."

"Well, let's get away from the door at least," said Polo.

"She's in class three," said Petrina as we walked toward Pavneet.

"Yeah, like I know. That's what I'm asking."

"Hello. Good morning. First day of school. Isn't this fun? I have to go back. We had a break. But it's over," said Pavneet. She was with Pippa and Prima.

Pavneet has lived in many different houses. She first lived with some very old pumpkins. And when they died, she moved. And then she moved again and again. Last year, she ended up with new housemates who were very mean to her. That's how she got sick on Halloween with rat poison. She lived right near me. Then she moved again a few months back. Her new housemates didn't seem much nicer. Now she lives near Portia.

"Hey, Prima," I said. I didn't talk to her much, so I thought I would say hello—you know, to keep the communication lines open, if there was ever a need. She has two brothers, Prime and Primo. Actually her real name is Primadonna, but it's too awkward to say. Even she thinks so. But she hasn't actually changed her name, like Pom Pom did. And it's Primodon and Primeodonnus. My goodness. Some pumpkins have the longest names.

They didn't have time to stay with us during our break. They ran back inside the building, along with the rest of their class.

"I want to talk to Picasso," I mentioned to Petrina. I wanted him to paint a real beautiful picture of the ocean, with the downtown skyline of New Surrey City as the backdrop. And it should be double the size he drew for Petrina. It just had to look much better.

"Well this is gonna suck. She isn't even in our class," lamented Petrina.

"I know, right?" added Pashelle. After a pause, she said, "How much time do we have?"

"Like fifteen minutes … ten minutes," I answered.

"What do you wanna do?"

"What can we do? We don't have much time. We don't have time to do anything."

"Let's play soccer," suggested Polo.

"Let's go to the playground and go down the slides."

"I'm too tired," I said. I really was. It was quite a frantic morning, running all the way to school. Even after all this time, I was still trying to catch my breath. My legs felt achy. Or was that due to sitting in that cramped desk?

"Let's just go sit down somewhere. We can sit on those swings. Or on that rubber tire."

The playground wasn't that far away from our classroom entrance. We slowly started walking. I spotted Patrick and Parson kicking a soccer ball back and forth. Parson was using his left foot. His right foot pinky toe must still be sore from the morning accident, no doubt. Polo and Pashelle stopped to join them, while Petrina, Plato, and I continued onward to the playground and eventually sat on the swings. We didn't sit on the swings for more than a few seconds before we started seeing our classmates go back inside.

"Okay, Pannette. That was fun. Let's go back inside," suggested Petrina.

And with those few words, it was time to go back inside. The walk back to the school building seemed longer than the one to the playground. There weren't many pumpkins on the school grounds. It seemed that our break came later than everyone else's.

"I thought Pickle and Pepper were older," Petrina remarked.

"What do you mean?" I asked.

"Didn't we have a birthday party for them? It was right around this time last year."

"Maybe. But they're the same age as us. They were born in the same summer."

"Pashelle said they were two years older."

"Don't listen to her. She was probably playing a trick on you. Did you ask either of them?"

"I don't know. Oh. My bad."

Once we were back inside, in our seats, Ms. Pumpkin started to go through our schedule for the foreseeable future. Every day we would take two fifteen-minute breaks and a full hour break for lunch. She explained what was expected of us—like not being late and not talking out of turn. Homework assignments needed to be completed properly and on time. School was important because … and she went on about that subject for a while. She gave us a brief description about each of our studies, which included math, history, English, fitness, technology, and on and on. Too many classes. She told us that each class would be taught by a master of that material. She referred to them as subject matter experts. She said we should view her as more of a guidance counselor rather than a teacher. All of that discussion, or lecture, took us to lunch, which we ate at the school cafeteria. We weren't really allowed to leave the school grounds, so there really wasn't much for us to do during breaks and lunches. I was sure we would just hang out and socialize. Before leaving school on that first day, we received our school bags. They were orange, of course. We were instructed to bring the bag with us every day.

School had started, and I was not looking forward to it. All the studying, and paying attention to Ms. Pumpkin and these so-called experts. What if my brain crashed due to an overload of information? My body would be sore, sitting cramped up in that desk. What a waste of time this was going to be. I would much rather be in the lounge, or just at home. I started to appreciate the early years of my life. I got the feeling that life was going to be much more difficult from now on.

CHAPTER 3
RULES

I t didn't take long for us to establish a daily routine. Essentially it meant getting up early in the morning, traveling to school, and listening to various elders give us lectures and training. The best part of school were the breaks and lunches. As the days went by, some of the five-year-olds started to run in the morning, including some of my closest friends. I went running with them one morning, and I ended up twisting my ankle. I stepped on a rock. My left foot became swollen on the back heel. I had to keep cold ice on it for two whole days. After school, we usually met up at the lounge. We spent less and less time at my house. Everyone always had homework to complete. Petrina spent a lot of time with Peter at the library. Pashelle spent a lot of time with Plato and Polo. Pavneet spent much of her time in a study group, which included Portia and Parker.

One day after school in the lounge, Pavneet was telling us about the things she did in her class. She went through her class schedule, including the lecture and training times, and her break and lunch times. We compared her schedule with ours.

Pavneet told us that each student had to rise out of his or her seat on that first day. One by one, each pumpkin had to stand up in front of the class and say something about him or herself—anything. Even the teacher did so. Ms. Pumpkin explained to the class how she obtained her necklace, the one with the beautifully carved white stones. Luckily, all we did was roll call.

We talked about all the rules we had to follow. We talked about all the homework we had to complete. I was disappointed that we were spending less and less time with each other in our usual setting, which was at my house.

"We can't even leave the school grounds. Too bad we can't come to the lounge during our lunch break." I continued on with my rant. "And Ms. Pumpkin is so mean. She's always getting mad at me. She pushes us so hard to do so many things."

"That's because you're always late. And you never do anything that you are supposed to do," observed Petrina.

I did. Well I thought I did. I mean, I did most of the things. I spent time on the farm the other day, helping with the vegetables. But wait. Did I go to the farm to help this week? I could not remember. I got so confused. There were so many things we had to do that it was difficult to keep track of them all. At least I spent time helping do clean-up in the supply center. Did I do that? Maybe I didn't. I opened my notebook that tracked my schedule of tasks, and it was listed. But there were no signatures of confirmation from the elders. So maybe I didn't. Oh that's right. I couldn't. I had to meet a friend in the lounge. Who cared anyways? Those tasks were not really important.

And we had so many rules. We got in trouble for everything.

"We don't get in trouble for everything, Pannette," said Plato.

"Yes we do," I replied.

Pashelle was on my side. She wanted to prove Plato wrong, almost. We were in the school cafeteria the next day.

"Are we allowed to take food out of the school cafeteria?" she asked Plato.

"No. I don't know," he replied.

"Well, I'm going to find out. I'm going to bring this apple with me," she whispered as she showed us the apple she was about to put in her sac.

"You can't," warned Polo.

"Why? Who said?"

"Mr. Pumpkin said," answered Polo.

"I don't think that is socially acceptable," added Pavneet.

"I know, right?"

"How come that's all you ever say?" wondered Pashelle as she stared at Polo.

"What?" Polo asked.

"Mr. Pumpkin said."

"Because he did."

"Seriously? It still doesn't make any sense."

"What?" I asked.

"What are you talking about?" Plato asked, wondering the same thing.

"I know, right?"

I got so confused. I lost track of our conversation.

"Well I don't care. I'm gonna take this apple with me," announced Pashelle.

"Aw!" I exclaimed. "You're gonna get in trouble."

"I might. Let's see if I do," said Pashelle.

"You might get detention."

"So. Who cares?"

"Like you really want to go to the office again and explain to the elders why you stole?"

"It's not stealing."

"Yes it is."

"No it isn't."

"Why do you want detention?"

"How is anyone going to know?"

"They check."

"No they don't."

"Yes they do."

I watched Pashelle slide an apple and a banana into her sac. Then she said, "Okay. Come on, everybody."

So we all got up and started walking casually toward the cafeteria exit. We were minding our own business. Maybe it was the guilty look on her face, or maybe someone saw her put the fruit in her sac, or maybe ... well, I don't know. But someone had alerted a security guard. While the rest of us were told to continue onward to our class, Pashelle was forced to stop. She had to empty out all her possessions from her sac. Pashelle was not happy. I don't know if her face turned red from rage or from embarrassment. We waited only a few more minutes outside the cafeteria entrance before we were ordered once more to return to class. Apparently we were blocking the doorway.

Pashelle never showed up for class that afternoon. Instead she told us what happened later that evening in the lounge.

"It was Portia. I know it was. Just before I was stopped, I saw her give me this smirky smile. As if to say, 'Gotcha.'"

"So where were you all day?"

"First I got taken to the office, and I had to meet with the elected elders. They asked me lots of questions. I told them that we should be allowed to take fruit from the school cafeteria. They didn't care though. I mean, why bother with the interrogation if they didn't even care what I said? After the questioning, Ms. Pumpkin escorted me to the restroom. She gave me a mop and a sponge and soap and water, and a bucket and whatever else."

I knew what she was going to say. We all did.

"Aw!" we exclaimed.

"I had to clean the restroom."

How gross is that.

"I had to clean inside the toilets, too. I almost threw up. The smell was disgusting. And she just stared and watched. She didn't lift a finger to help. 'This is good for you, Pashelle,' she said."

"But you were gone for hours. How long did it take?"

"I was allowed to go home after. I needed to take a bath. I smelled gross. I mean, there was no way I was coming back to the school. And when Paxton and Payne came home from school, they started teasing me."

Paxton and Payne were two of her four older brothers.

"Trust me. It's not the same thing as cleaning your own toilet."

"I told you," said Petrina.

"Well geez, Petrina. I didn't figure you to be the 'I told you so' type."

I did. Petrina was definitely the "I told you so" type.

"I hate Portia. I'm gonna get her back. I swear I will. And that Paige … I could picture all of them laughing at me. As I was cleaning, Paige came into the restroom and made a mess on purpose."

That sounded ugly.

"What do you mean she made a mess?" I asked. I couldn't imagine.

"She spilled water on the floor and didn't even throw her dirty paper towels in the garbage can."

"Recycling container," corrected Pavneet.

"What?"

"It's called recycling."

"We recycle dirty washroom towels? Like no way." I was surprised.

"I don't know. But it's still called the recycling container. We're not supposed to say garbage can. It's not socially acceptable."

I could empathize with Pashelle. I mean, we had so many rules we had to follow. It was ridiculous. We were not allowed to do anything. And some of the rules were so silly.

For instance, a few weeks later, I was asked to help Ms. Pumpkin with the sorting of the bed sheets after laundry day. I had to put each of them in specific piles. I started to get confused, and some of the sheets ended up in the incorrect pile. This was discovered after the laundry delivery, when some pumpkins complained they got the wrong bed sheets.

But who cared? What difference did it make that some pumpkins received different bed covers? They were all the same, weren't they? Some pumpkins even complained to the elected elders that the five-year-olds were lacking discipline and a sense of responsibility—that school had become too "soft" and we were given too much freedom and choice. Like, are you kidding me? Too much freedom and choice? The nerve.

"It wasn't like that in our day, Patten," I overheard two elders.

"I know. The pumpkins of today lack structure," replied Patten. "That is the problem. Do you remember when we had to take defense training?"

"Yes. Yes." The other elder nodded in agreement. "Didn't Pavlov do a study confirming that pumpkins worked just as hard as ants? And now look how far behind we are."

"What would we do if we were ever attacked? We would stand no chance. No chance at all. The pumpkins wouldn't even know how to defend ourselves. We would be like sitting ducks out here. We need to get pumpkins more physically fit. We need to get back to basics and have all the pumpkins take part in some kind of military training."

Military training. Patten Pumpkin wanted us to take military training? My goodness. I was not sure if I could handle that.

And what type of rule determined which pumpkin sat in which class? No one could explain how, at the last minute, Pavneet was moved to class 3. And as a result, we spent even less time with her. We didn't have very much interaction with the other two classes. Luckily, though, when we did, I was often paired with Pavneet during demonstrations and communication exercises. One time we had to draw a picture of each other in art class. For the most part, though, we only interacted with our own class—something that caused Petrina much annoyance. She was often paired up with Palmer. She had complained about it many times. She had a distrust of Palmer.

"I don't like him!" she said more than once. "I don't like sitting next to him. He's always staring at me."

We were later told that Pavneet's move to class 3 may have been a clerical error. A typo. And we found out there was another clerical error. Actually this one was labeled as a "miscommunication" by the school committee. Pippa and Pippi should have been in the same class, because they were sisters. The elders intended to keep brothers and sisters in the same class. There were rules for everything. Pippa had finally become fed up with Panic and his childish antics. "Too many practical jokes," Pippa said. Panic could get so hyper. Not even a talk with Ms. Pumpkin could subdue him. Pippa wanted a permanent solution to the problem. She wanted a change of scenery. She wanted to sit with her sister. Petrina saw this as an opportunity for herself. She thought with this pending class shuffle, it was best if Palmer was the one to be switched out. The elders were going to ensure there were an equal number of students in each class, no doubt. Petrina needed to devise a plan. She was willing to do anything to break up the partnership.

"When Ms. Pumpkin asks for a volunteer to leave the class, and you know she will, we need to ensure that Palmer volunteers," she demanded.

"What do you mean by 'we'? And how are we going to get him to volunteer?"

"Ummm, let me think. I know. No. Wait. You think of something, Pannette."

"I don't know. Palmer can write a note to Ms. Pumpkin."

"Why?"

"To say that he wants to move," I explained.

"Yes. Right. And you're going to write it for him."

"Why me?"

"Because it was your idea. And you have neater handwriting. Besides, if something goes wrong they will naturally suspect me, mainly because of all my complaints about him. But they would never suspect you."

Petrina thought I had neat handwriting? Sure. I bet she did. I would only get a compliment from Petrina when she had an ulterior motive.

And so I thought, *Whatever. Why not? We've done worse things. Besides, I don't want to move. I don't want to be voluntold. Better Palmer moves than me.*

We thought about the ways we could get a sample of his writing. The best idea we came up with was to steal some of his homework. Petrina would distract him, and I would steal papers from his desk or from his school bag.

For the next few days, we tried. But for whatever reason, we were not successful. We knew that time was running out. Sometimes there were too many pumpkins watching or near enough to notice. Sometimes he didn't have any writings close at hand or that were easily visible. I mean, both of them sat right near the door, and they were seated right in front of Ms. Pumpkin in the first row. Just as our morning break started one day, he left papers open on his desk and went out the door in a rush—maybe to use the toilet. Who knows? But then Ms. Pumpkin was eyeing us, so we couldn't take any action at that time, either.

We had decided this plan was not going to work.

"We need another plan, Pannette," she said desperately. "Ms. Pumpkin is going to decide on a volunteer soon, and we have nothing."

I was thinking, *Why don't you get a life, Petrina?* And Petrina was getting annoyed by the day, having to engage in idle conversation with Palmer. She was thinking about him all the time. She had become accustomed to his movements and habits. She became familiar with his voice and speaking style.

This was later confirmed. Palmer came up to me in the lounge one evening, and he asked me if I wanted a drink.

"Sure, Palmer. Why don't you get me an orange juice?" I answered.

He came back with a fresh orange juice from the bar.

"I think Petrina is starting to like me, Pannette. She seems to be spending so much time with me. She is so interested, asking me all kinds of questions."

That's when I came up with a better idea.

"Write her a note, Palmer!" I blurted out.

"A note?"

"Yes. A note. Share your feelings with her. Make your intentions known."

"I wouldn't know what to write. What would I write?"

"Anything. Anything at all. Anything you feel like saying to her. And I can even read it over for you. You know, to ensure she would like it."

"I don't know, Pannette. Why write a note when I sit right next to her in class?"

"Sure. Sure. This is it. This is a better idea. I mean, this is the best thing for you to do. Come on, Palmer. Write something. Do you have any paper?"

I saw Penelope with a pad and pencil and raced over to ask for help. I returned with all the supplies Palmer would need.

"Here. Write something."

He proceeded to write the most beautiful, poetic note to Petrina. He wrote about his desire to be with her, that she was the only pumpkin he wanted to spend time and have a conversation with. It didn't take him long to write the note at all.

"This is really nice, Palmer." I hoped someone would write a letter like this for me one day. Palmer must read a lot of poetry.

"Do you read poetry?" I inquired.

"I don't know. Not really," he answered. "Okay then. I will give this to her tomorrow."

"No. Wait. Let me read it some more. Let me take it home with me. I will give it back to you tomorrow. Let me see if I have further suggestions. This is going to be our secret, okay?" I didn't want him blabbing all over the patch about this letter.

That evening, when I got home, I practiced his writing style over and over again, all of the nuances of his writing. The way he dotted the Is and crossed the Ts. How curved his letters were. And then I wrote a note to Ms. Pumpkin, expressing his desire to change classes, on his behalf. It was signed Palmer Pumpkin.

"What are you doing?" asked Patrick.

"Nothing."

I had to be careful. I quickly put some other papers over the letter. I didn't want to create any suspicion at all.

"Don't tell me you're doing homework. Since when?"

"I am. I am. Really. I'm writing a story."

The very next day during the morning break, I told Petrina how I was able to secure a piece of paper with his handwriting. I showed her the note I wrote. She thought it was wonderful. Thank you very much. I never did show her or tell her about the note Palmer wrote.

"How are we going to give this note to Ms. Pumpkin?" she asked.

I thought for a second. And then there she was, just outside the door. I thought we should put it on her desk. "Like right now," I said. We hurried back into class and finished the job.

And would you believe the very next day, it was announced that Palmer and Pippa were changing classes. Palmer must have been so dejected. Petrina would be elated. I considered it a plan executed to perfection.

As for the love letter? I couldn't give it to Petrina. It would put her in a difficult positon. It would have freaked her out. I had to give it back to Palmer. And I did.

"Maybe now is not the best time, Palmer, especially with you moving to a different class. A change of scenery can alter the circumstances," I explained.

I thought to myself, *What have I done? Have I permanently tarnished their relationship? Have I just ruined any chance of them being really good friends? Poor Palmer. Have I just given him the worst advice ever? I'm sure I broke some kind of rule. Oh well. It was still a perfectly executed plan.*

At the end of the first month of school, Ms. Pumpkin had a meeting with me. She summoned me to the classroom early one morning. She wanted to have a meeting and discuss my progress at school. She called it a one-on-one meeting. She didn't waste any time. She expressed her disappointment in my performance. I was like, *What? Where did this come from?* I was taken aback. She told me that I was underperforming, and she wanted more effort.

I was shocked. I thought I was doing well, and here she was

getting on my case about performance and work habits. She said I was lagging behind all the other pumpkins. She wanted me to ensure that I fulfilled my responsibilities and that I followed the rules. There we go again with the rules.

"I've done everything, Ms. Pumpkin," I said in my defense.

"Well, I know you can do better," was her reply.

She said we would meet again the following month, and we would continue on with this discussion. She reminded me of my task for the next morning, and then dismissed me.

"Okay. You can go now. Take a short break because the classes don't start for another twenty minutes," she ordered.

Well excuse me, I thought to myself as I slowly left the room. She put me in such a bad mood that I didn't talk to my friends the whole day. The whole day! That's how much I was disgusted with Ms. Pumpkin. It ended up being a long day. I wanted to forget about the whole incident, so I pretended like the meeting didn't happen. It was a waste of time, that's all.

The next day was a holiday. It was a teachers' holiday. Wow. Good for them. They get a holiday. I guess she needed time to recuperate from all the nasty things she said to me. That one-on-one meeting was ugly. But today was going to be a better day.

I was in the lounge that afternoon. I had nothing to do except to enjoy my favorite pastime, which was doing nothing. Almost all of the five-year-olds were in the lounge. As the other pumpkins were participating in idle chatter, I spent the afternoon watching Mr. Pumpkin trying to organize something. We called him the bartender. He spent his time preparing drinks for us. He kept himself busy behind the bar counter, sometimes pouring drinks for the pumpkins, sometimes cleaning, washing, then drying and putting the dishes neatly on the counter. He always made sure there was enough ice available. He was a very social pumpkin. He loved to share his feelings and was always providing advice to other pumpkins. That afternoon, he kept looking down the hall, toward the entrance, as if he were waiting for something to happen. I'm not sure why. Maybe he lost something. Just then, I noticed Peter and Petrina come into the lounge, and they started having a conversation with him. All three of them seemed concerned. I wondered what the issue was. I summoned Petrina over toward me.

"What's going on with Mr. Pumpkin?" I asked.

"It's Ms. Pumpkin's birthday today, and Mr. Pumpkin wants to do something special. He wants to throw a surprise birthday party for her."

"And ...?"

"He wants to surprise her right now. But he was supposed to have received a new shipment of utensils. You know. Like knives, spoons, forks—"

"Yeah. I know what utensils are."

"Well, he doesn't have any. So now no one can eat the birthday cake properly, without the utensils. So he may go to the supply center himself because Ms. Pumpkin has to go to the greenhouse really soon."

Wait a minute. That's what I was supposed to do this morning. I was supposed to go to the supply center and bring a package back to the lounge. Oh no. I didn't want to ruin the birthday party. I leapt from my seat and hurried toward the lounge exit.

"I will get them. I will get the utensils!" I yelled to Mr. Pumpkin as I left the lounge in a panic.

We had to run so many errands for the elders. Go to the supply center, and help Mr. Pumpkin with this. Go to the kitchen, and help Ms. Pumpkin with that. It was difficult to keep up with all the things they make us perform.

As I was walking to the supply center, running almost, I did recall that I had asked Peter to do me a favor. And he said he would. He was the one who was supposed to go and run this errand. He promised me he would, so this was all his fault. I was breaking my back, trying to make things right. Why did he say he would do me this favor if he wasn't going to carry it out?

By the time I reached the supply center, I had become irate with Peter.

Mr. Pumpkin let me in and gave me the box. He was expecting me, he said. I didn't have time to chat with him, though. It seemed a longer walk back. I had to rest. I was tired from this incredibly long, quick sprint. I sat on a rose garden bench for a few minutes. But just as I was eager to return to the lounge to yell at Peter, I wanted to get the utensils to Mr. Pumpkin, so I didn't rest for very long.

However, by the time I got back to the lounge, Ms. Pumpkin had already left for the greenhouse.

"That's okay, Pannette. Thank you so much for bringing these. We sure do need them," Mr. Pumpkin said.

"Did we cut her birthday cake?"

"Yes, we did. I used this knife, and she used this same one to eat her piece. But since none of us could eat the other pieces, she took her cake to the greenhouse with her. They have plates and spoons over there, and she can feed the other pumpkins at the greenhouse. They would appreciate that, I'm sure," he explained.

Where was Peter? Where was he? I looked around, but I didn't see him. Of course, he probably took off. He knew he did something wrong. And now he doesn't want to face me. No worries. I will see him when I see him. He can't hide forever.

In the meantime, I decided to let go of the issue. After all, today was going to be a better day. It was unfortunate that pumpkins didn't get to taste the birthday cake. But there would be other occasions, no doubt.

CHAPTER 4
THE LOUNGE

On Saturday there was no school. No school on the weekends. That was a relief. I decided to spend my day in the lounge. This was where all of us had been spending so much of our time, apart from school. We used to spend a lot of time at my house, but not so much these days.

The lounge was such a nice and cozy place. It made one feel very welcome. It was one of the few areas in the patch made of wood. I am not sure why. Maybe we wanted to do something different. All the houses, and most of the other buildings, were brick. The newly added west wing in the school was made of wood. The lounge was also the newest place. It was a recent extension of the activity center building. The roof was shaped like a point. On one side of the room were the pool tables, dart boards, and a serving bar. There were lots of different types of drinks behind this bar—some alcoholic, some not. I was too young to be served the alcoholic ones. There was a small kitchen, with an oven behind the bar counter. We could order simple food, like French fries, sandwiches, or hamburgers. On another side of the lounge, there was a quiet sitting area, with coffee tables and couches to carry out conversation. It had a nice view of the daffodil garden. And on another side of the lounge, there were televisions. We had three of them. Two of them were twenty inches across, while the third was fifty-two inches. That television was very large. It was hung up on the wall. The lounge had hardwood floors.

In the lounge, there was no shortage of things to do. Parties and celebrations were held. On these occasions we had fancy meals. Well, not me. I was too young for that. I'd never been served a fancy meal.

The only downside of the lounge was that it was too small. It needed to be enlarged. There were only enough seats for about fifty pumpkins. Once you found a seat, you didn't want to get up and vacate it because that likely meant standing or leaning against a wall. And it was very cramped. You couldn't move two feet without running into someone. It could get crowded in a hurry. It could take someone forever to travel from the sitting area to the bar, or to the television room. It was usually the busiest after dinner and all day on the weekends. And it was no different on this day. The place was hopping, abuzz with excitement. There was always some big event going on. The table tennis final was happening in the arena later. I knew that. And the darts and pool table finals were today as well—just for the five-year-olds. Next weekend, it would be the finals for the six-year-olds. I'm sure the following weekend would be the finals for the seven-year-olds.

Sometimes pumpkins would crank up the music and have a dance party, much to the chagrin of the elders quietly reading in the sitting area. They even complained the televisions could be too loud.

"Turn it down. Why is it so loud?" Ms. Pumpkin asked that day as she entered the television room. The room was not really a room with walls. It was separated from the bar, only because the couches and chairs faced inward, toward the large television, which created a border. Ms. Pumpkin had an open book in her left hand, peering around the room, looking for the remote control, no doubt. But in all honesty, I doubt anyone paid any attention to her. I was sure of it. There was too much chatter in the television room. Even the pumpkins who wanted to watch television couldn't, because of the noise. I heard her only because I was sitting down on the couch, near the room entrance. And it wasn't just the noise of the televisions that bothered her. The pumpkins in the bar were just as noisy.

We could hear Mr. Pumpkin yell out numbers over the microphone: sixty-five, forty-one, sixteen. And he got more excited as the number became larger. "One hundred and forty!" he screamed. That announcement was met with a small roar. That must have been a great shot. The darts final was going on. I was not even sure who was playing. I lost to Prime in the first round, a few months back.

"Who's playing in the darts final?" I asked of no one in particular.

No one answered—not even Peanut, who was sitting right next to me.

She was talking about the news. I mean the news, from the people we see on television and read about in the newspapers. She was talking about the violence and other crime that occurred every day in the city.

"It's every day. It's sickening, the way people treat each other. And for what? And their police are so overworked, and—" she explained to Porter and Penny.

The pumpkins across from me didn't hear me either. Prudence, Pandria, and Pluto were talking about Halloween costumes. Halloween was fast approaching.

There was an argument going on about the use of the television itself. The one that was hung on the wall. Paris and Paige wanted to watch a musical contest, while Pretty wanted to watch a fashion show. I'm sure of it. I could see them getting animated and lively.

"It's the semifinals. It's not fair. You can watch *American Idol* whenever you want. It comes on every day," is what Pretty would have said. I could see them yelling at each other, for at least ten minutes.

"Paris dear, let Pretty watch." I'm sure that's what Ms. Pumpkin said to them, as she had to intervene. I was too far away to actually hear them.

Way on the other side of the room, I saw Petrina wave. Why? She was almost jumping up and down in her seat. And I could see her scream out, "Pannette! Pannette!"

Oh! One of the pumpkins over there was leaving. Good. Finally I could sit down next to my friends. But before I did that, I had to get closer and listen to the rest of the television fight.

"But we reserved it, Ms. Pumpkin. I didn't get to watch the last time I reserved the television either. Mr. Pumpkin let Petunia watch. Then what is the point of making a reservation?" said Paige.

She had a good point. A television schedule was drawn out. More rules. It was girls' night out in the lounge today. That meant the main television was reserved for girls. One of the twenty-inch televisions was always reserved for the elders. The third television was always on a news channel, like CNN.

I squeezed in between Petrina and Pavneet on a couch. There were a lot of pumpkins crowded around.

"What's going on over there?" I was asked.

"They're fighting over the television. So what's new?" I replied.

"Do you know we are getting another television?" said Patience.

"Yeah, I heard that too. It's a donation from the United Way," said Pickle.

We got many donations from the United Way, but it was rare that we got electronics from them.

"Why are they giving us a television? How did they get one?" I asked.

"Because someone gave it to them."

"Ms. Pumpkin says that's only going to be used for PlayStation or Xbox."

"Who said?"

"I just said. Ms. Pumpkin."

"That's a good idea."

"Computer games are getting so popular, aren't they?"

"Parker wants to have a tournament of some kind, just like we do with other things that go on in here."

"And Wii?"

"I guess—if you want to play with them."

"You're not very good, anyway. So why do you want to play?" teased Prima.

"No. Not us. Well maybe. I don't know. But I said Wii, for PlayStation," replied Polo.

"You said 'we.'"

"I said Wii."

"What's that?"

"Yeah. What is that?" I was curious too.

"Don't you know anything?"

What? What did Petrina just say to me?

"There's no room in here for another television," reasoned Plato. "The square footage of the lounge is—"

"I know right," interrupted Pashelle.

"They might put it in the arena."

"At least we're getting one."

"Who would be crazy enough to go to the arena just to play a computer game?" I said. "I mean, it would be so much nicer in here."

"I'm better than you," stated Polo.

"Oh. No way. You haven't even seen me play. I'm really good at Tetris." Prima seemed to have taken exception to the implication.

"That's not a real game. Have you ever played Madden?" asked Polo.

"I haven't even heard of that game," Prima said in her defense.

It seemed that more arguments were happening over the use of the televisions, especially since the elders had added a bunch of movie channels to our package.

"I heard that we are getting a subscription to the NFL Sunday Ticket, and the NHL Center Ice package next year," said Polo with a gleaming face.

"I heard that too," said Peyton, who happened to catch Polo's excitement.

"Looks like we're going to need more televisions."

"That is kind of boring," said Pavneet. Not a surprise she would say that. She was a very outdoor type of person. She didn't like sitting in closed spaces. Even sitting in the lounge, with all these pumpkins crowded together can be an annoyance for her.

I am more of an indoors type of person. I like sitting in the lounge and having a rest. I enjoy watching. There's always something to watch.

"Why are we talking about television anyway?" questioned Pavneet.

"Oh! Did you hear about Walden Werewolf?"

"I did. Papi told me."

"It's Mr. Pumpkin! Mr. Pumpkin. What is your problem?" I'd had to correct Petrina like so many times now. She could be so dense. Papi Pumpkin was an elder. We were not supposed to call elders by their given names. We had to say Mr. or Ms., but Petrina couldn't seem to let go of "Papi."

"I don't have a problem. What's your problem?"

Petrina squinted her eyes and gave me a rude stare. She has such a big ego. Such a drama queen. And she is always ordering me around. She was still staring at me, while Pashelle was waving at us. She wanted to finish her story.

"No, listen. But did you hear what happened at the funeral?" Pashelle continued.

"What funeral?"

"He died."

"Aw!"

"Why? What happened at the funeral?"

"Where was the funeral?"

"Probably on the dark side of the moon."

"How do you know?"

"What's a funeral?"

"Do you know how he died?"

"I didn't think werewolves could die."

"No, listen. Some werewolves spotted a mysterious ghoul. It was right in the front, at the same time they were administering the sacred oath to William. That ghoul was not supposed to be there. They don't know how this ghoul could have slipped through their security. It was only seen afterward, when they were reviewing the film. They say this could pose a dangerous risk. The werewolves are worried this ghoul may now have access to certain privileged information or something."

"What information?" I asked.

"What could the ghoul do?"

"Who is William?"

"William Werewolf is now the new leader of all werewolves."

"How do you know this?"

"Well no one knows for sure," answered Pashelle.

"Well, you don't know for sure."

"Who told you this?"

"I have my sources."

"Yeah, who?"

"Why? Why do I have to reveal my sources?"

"Wait, what new information?" I asked.

I missed that part. All my friends talked so fast. Sometimes it was hard to follow the conversation. It's like, what did she say? Then what did he say? I ended up saying, "What?" many times. I would get so confused. Then I started thinking about what I may have missed. And because I went into this deep thought, I ended up missing out on the rest of the conversation.

"What? What new information?" I asked again.

"It was a scary night," explained Pashelle.

"How do you know it was a scary night?"

"Were you there?" I asked. I was sure Pashelle was making some of this stuff up as she went along.

"It must have been scary. It was a werewolf funeral," she reasoned. "What type of night do you think it was?"

"Have you ever been to a werewolf funeral? Then why would you think it was scary?"

"What is a funeral?" Polo was still waiting for his question to be answered. He didn't even know what a funeral was.

"It was probably a vampire. What else could it have been?"

"What if it was Wanda?"

Now that was a scary thought. Wanda Witch was our number one enemy. None of the pumpkins trusted her. She wanted to get rid of us all. She became the leader of the witches during the War of the Broomsticks. She probably had lots of powers. Now were we saying she may have acquired another one?

"I don't believe you," someone finally concluded.

Pashelle felt compelled to provide more detail.

"Okay. I'll tell you. When I was in the office for the whole food-sampling incident, I overheard the elected elders. They were trying to get more details as to what may have happened. But even they didn't know."

"What food-sampling incident? Do you mean when you smuggled food out of the school cafeteria?"

My goodness. Was it true? I wondered what new information this ghoul might have. I wondered if the ghoul obtained more power.

"What if this creates a new war?"

"That's all they do. They fight," added Plato. "I was reading the other day, in advance of species class. I was reading the new book, *The Witches War*. It was written by Victor Vampire. It was his first public account of the War of the Broomsticks."

There are many books written about that war. I haven't read any of them though.

"In the final chapter, he lists all the reasons why Wanda should have stood trial before the international tribunal. He says that many ghouls agree with him. Many ghouls think the witches got a sweetheart of a deal. Wanda Witch got everything she wanted. Many vampires didn't think this was right. There were pages and pages of a speech that Victor Vampire orated in their annual meeting and how he thought that everyone was too soft on her. Apparently this speech was given a long time ago but was only made public in this book. He wanted the war to continue, so that Wanda would eventually be defeated. But since people had so much desire for peace, they were willing to end it at all costs. He felt forced to instruct the vampire nation to accept the terms. They had no choice but to close the book on it. Everyone wanted the war to end. He wasn't happy at all. No ghoul was. He wanted to keep fighting."

That was interesting.

"No one likes Wanda Witch."

"I know, right?"

We were noticing the lounge was starting to clear. Pumpkins were leaving in groups.

"Where is everyone going?"

"Probably to the arena."

"Oh ... it's the table tennis final."

"Yeah," confirmed Pavneet. "That's supposed to start soon."

"Do we want to watch?"

"I do. It's exciting," claimed Petrina.

Just then Mr. Pumpkin came by and said he was disappointed in us. He said we should have all been near the darts board and pool table for the five-year-old finals. Instead we were here. We should have been there cheering them on.

"You should all go and stretch your legs," he said, and left to gather up more pumpkins. He was trying to get everyone in a fun and competitive spirit. He wanted us to watch the table tennis final.

"It's so nice here. I'm so comfortable. We have seats," I pleaded to my friends. But no one really listened to me.

"Well, if we are going to watch, then we might as well go now, so we can get close to the table. Or else we won't be able to see anything. Come on, everybody," Pashelle instructed. She got up, expecting us all to follow, and follow we did. We went out the side door of the lounge, passed through the carnation garden, and entered the arena.

The arena was the largest building in the patch. There was enough room to cram in almost a thousand pumpkins. There was more than enough space. I didn't even think there were that many pumpkins in this patch. It was made of brick. The ground was all natural grass—none of that artificial grass people have in their arenas. It was used for many functions, like meetings, announcements, and sporting events. The Halloween party would be there.

The table tennis table was situated on the stage, at the front, and so we tried pushing our way closer toward the table. But we really didn't get close. Too many pumpkins were in front of us. It was going to be difficult to see the table tennis ball properly, if I cared. In the final, it was Pong Pumpkin versus Ping Pumpkin. I had lost to Pong in the first round, about two months prior. I'm not even sure if I won a single point in any of our games. He had super reflexes—I could tell you that. He made quick work out of me. He probably didn't even work up a sweat. My wrist started to hurt a few minutes into the second game. To be honest, I had no chance—like no chance at all.

We gave up pushing our way toward the front and decided to move off to the side and sit down.

While the finalists were in their pregame warmup, Poker sat down next to Pashelle and asked her if she wanted to play cards. "I'll show you a different game," he said. He gave her five cards and asked her if they had anything in common. "Are they all the same, or are they in a sequence, or are they in the same suit?" he asked.

He wanted to teach her a new game. Pashelle seemed excited. I was just watching them. I was bored. I didn't have anything else to do. Pavneet and Petrina started talking with Pebbles and Peanut to my left. Porter and Peter were also in that conversation. They were talking about some kind of contest that was going to occur. I was kind of half listening to them, while also listening to Patience and Penny, who were standing, almost hovering over me. They were talking about their Halloween costumes. Prime and Primo were sitting to my right, and they were going on about a stunt that Panic and Perses wanted to pull off during class one day.

"It's never going to work," said Primo.

So many different conversations were going on around me. It seemed I was involved in all of them, listening intently. But in reality, I wasn't in any of them. I didn't know who to pay attention to. I had such a short attention span. And pumpkins can talk so fast. I could hear other pumpkins talking about the death of Walden Werewolf and what this could mean for us.

"What if William turns out to be like Wanda and wants to exterminate us all?" asked Pauline.

"A change like this could upset the balance of power," remarked Pacino.

Just as Poker told Pashelle that she had lost the card game, Mr. Pumpkin was speaking into the microphone, instructing everyone to quiet down. Pashelle started to get upset. She didn't think she lost. Poker was insisting that Pashelle take off her red bow from her stem. Pashelle wanted to know why. Why did Pashelle have to take off her red bow? And just as the arena became all quiet, Poker and Pashelle started to raise their voices. Poker was insistent.

"Take off your red bow," he ordered.

And by the time the arena became dead quiet. All anyone heard was Pashelle.

"I'm not taking it off!" she screamed in her loudest voice.

The scream echoed throughout the arena. It was loud. Everyone had heard. Everyone was staring at us. Pashelle's face turned all red. That must have been embarrassing. I mean if I was her, I wouldn't take off my bow either. Just because she lost in a game of cards?

"All right now. No one is taking anything off," said Mr. Pumpkin. "Let's all relax."

That comment from Mr. Pumpkin caused a light-hearted laugh from the pumpkin crowd.

So the table tennis final had finally started. To be honest, I couldn't wait for it to end. I couldn't see any of the action sitting down. We weren't allowed to talk. The match lasted almost two hours. It was so boring, and I was so uninterested that I cannot even tell you who won. I'm sure this is disappointing, but I have very little interest in sports and games. I mean, who cares who won?

When the match was over, we all decided to return to the lounge. We were going to talk about the contest. Maybe one of us could win. Prudence was telling everyone within earshot that she had a great idea. It could be the winner. She didn't share the idea though. And I was like, *What contest?*

Pashelle and Pom Pom had a great idea too. So did Peter.

"Hey, Petrina. What contest? Do we have any ideas?" I had to shake her shoulders to force her attention toward me.

"No, not really," she responded. "We can think about it."

Okay, I thought. But I still didn't know what the contest was about.

We left the arena and headed back to the lounge. I doubted very much we were going to find any seats. Hurray for table tennis. That was a sarcastic thought. So we stood in the lounge, watching television, and congratulated the three winners of today's tournaments. Pong won the table tennis tournament. He also had won the pool tournament earlier. He defeated Pebbles in the final. Plunder was the winner of the darts final.

After the winners' ceremony, many of my friends decided to go to the dining hall and eat dinner. After dinner, it was decided that we should all go home. Some pumpkins wanted to study. Everyone thought it was a long day. I thought it was a short day. There was no school, and we were free to do anything we wanted. We were together in the lounge, having fun. I didn't feel like going home, but I did.

I stopped to chat with Peaches and Pillow, who were outside their door. They are my neighbors to the north. They are both four years old. They live with three very old pumpkins. I've known them almost my whole life. We are great friends. I share many things with them. I treat them as if they are my younger sisters, since I don't have any myself. They were talking about their Halloween costumes.

This year was going to be their first time trick or treating. It would be my second time. They were really nervous. They were giddy with excitement.

"Are you two going out together?" I wondered.

"Yes," replied Pillow.

"Actually, Pannette, we have been meaning to ask you. Is it okay if we come with you?" asked Peaches.

"Sure it is. It will be fun," I replied. The more the merrier. I told them what a great experience it would be. And all the candy!

By the time I went back inside my house, the weather had turned. It was cold. There was a northern wind that was hitting my face. That could only mean one thing—Halloween was just around the corner.

CHAPTER 5
HALLOWEEN

"What does Halloween mean to you?" asked Ms. Pumpkin one day.

Halloween is a big deal for us pumpkins—I mean a *really* huge deal. Our whole yearly schedule is based on and around Halloween. It's a tradition that dates back centuries. We think about it, plan it, and prepare for it. And of course we go trick or treating and collect mountains of candy. I would daydream about it. Last year was a riot. We brought home lots of candy. It was scary too. Pavneet was snatched up by witches and had to be saved. It's true. And we went inside a person's house. She was chasing after us with a huge knife. That was ugly. Some old lady told us that she was going to feed us freshly baked chocolate chip cookies, so we went inside her house to wait. Bad idea. When she came out of the kitchen, she wanted to carve us up. She wanted to turn us into pumpkin pies. We were running around the house, looking for a way out. We barely made it out of there alive. We ended up smashing a window near the front door after the lady hit a wall post and knocked herself out. Pashelle wanted to light her on fire. Well, I can assure you that we are not going into anyone's house this year.

We started studying for the trick or treat test. Yes, more homework. But that test was easy. Everyone passed.

One day in class, when I had stopped daydreaming, Ms. Pumpkin was handing out our schedules for Halloween preparation. Our duty was to decorate the arena. That's what we did last year too.

Ms. Pumpkin also said that Halloween was a good time to start species study. We had to study and learn the characteristics and physical traits of all different types of species—not in detail, but just the basics. Actually all of our classes during our first year of school were just the basics of pumpkin history, math, computers, and so on, including basic study of species.

She gave us each a copy of a manual. It was called *Species: A Beginner's Guide*, written by Pavlov Pumpkin. Apparently he had spent his entire life studying different types of species. How exciting for him. She told us to open the manual to the first page, and we were going to look at the table of contents.

Table of Contents
Module 1: Ants and Other Insects
Module 2: Birds
Module 3: Cats
Module 4: Dogs
Module 5: Ghosts
Module 6: People (Apes, Gorillas, and Monkeys)
Module 7: Squash
Module 8: Vampires (and Bats)
Module 9: Werewolves
Module 10: Witches and Warlocks

She said we would skip module 1. We didn't need to learn

about ants. She also said we would study fish and other aquatic life sometime next year. That we may visit a park near Burrowsville. There are separate study materials for fish. And if there was time, our studies would include rats, mice, and other vermin. Snakes and other reptiles were for later school years. We would also skip module 7, as she felt it would be a waste of our time. Like, isn't all of this a waste of our time?

"Why are vampires and bats in the same module?" I asked Peter.

"Just pay attention to Ms. Pumpkin," he answered. "She will tell you everything you need to know. Try and focus."

"There is no talking during teacher instruction, Peter. You know that," said Ms. Pumpkin.

Peter turned and gave me an awkward look. His big eyes stuck out from his glasses. Very few pumpkins had to wear glasses. He must have been as blind as a bat.

"Are bats blind?" I asked him again.

This time he didn't answer me. He just completely ignored me. He can be that way sometimes. He can be very unsocial. Yet other times, he can be the life of a party. His behavior can be a bit erratic—very unpredictable. You never know what you're going to get from him. Sometimes he's nice, and other times he can be a goof. Sometimes he can be so funny, while other times very stoic and boring. He acts so strange. You can't even tell if he's joking or serious. He has like ten different personalities in his body, and he picks and chooses the one he wants in any given day.

Oh here I go, daydreaming again. The next thing I heard was, "Pannette, are you paying attention?"

"Yes, Ms. Pumpkin," I replied.

"Who is Count Dracula?"

I don't know. How would I know? Why doesn't she tell me? All I could do was shrug my shoulders.

Then she started shaking her head. "I think it's time for a break," she said in frustration. *Good*, I thought, *because I need a break.* My head was starting to hurt.

Over the next several weeks, we went through each module, with a different teacher instructing us for each module. How boring. We studied the characteristics and attributes of each species. Their tendencies and ways of life. Eating and sleeping habits. Their physical traits, and what they look like. The colors of their skin. We were given additional manuals that had pictures so we would be able to identify each species. We learned about their language and the sounds and noises they made. We studied their origins and history. All of this was very important, we were told. If we studied them, then we would be more prepared to protect ourselves, if such a situation arose. We were told that all species were a danger to pumpkins.

"We must assume that all species enjoy pumpkin pie!" she warned.

We studied birds first. We learned about all the different types of birds. We spent a lot of time on crows and ravens, as we were most likely to meet them. Most birds fly. Chickens don't fly. Neither do turkeys. The most fascinating bird to me was the eagle. It has an incredible wingspan and can soar way up into the sky. And there are many different types of eagles. There is the bald eagle, the golden eagle, the white-tailed eagle, the stellar eagle, the sea eagle, and so on.

"Can eagles fly to the moon?" asked Pashelle.

"That has not yet been documented. Although, they certainly wouldn't want to disrespect the werewolves."

Then we studied cats. There are house cats and dangerous cats. Dangerous cats are kept in a zoo, while house cats live with people. There are other violent cats that live in the jungle, out in the wild. We studied lions, tigers, pumas, and leopards—all kinds of cats. The study of the dangerous cats was more interesting, as house cats don't seem to do much except sleep, eat, and drink.

Then we studied dogs.

"Do we get to learn dog language, Ms. Pumpkin?" asked Petrina one day.

"No. Only people learn dog language. We have asked people for a more detailed study of their language, but my understanding is we are still waiting for a response to that inquiry."

"Why?"

"Well, it has been discovered that dogs trust people. They only share with them. They have become best friends. Dogs don't trust any other species. It is our understanding that dogs have only provided certain details with people, with the trust that their language be kept secret."

I guess they are like pumpkins, because we don't trust any other species either.

One afternoon, Mr. Pumpkin came into the classroom and started talking about ghosts. "Ghosts are invisible. They can only be seen by other ghosts. They do not have a physical body. Since they do not have a physical body, growth and aging are not applicable for ghosts." The module explained the death of ghosts and their spiritual level.

"The pureness of their spirituality will determine the amount of energy they possess. As there is no physical body, there is no requirement for sleep, rest, or food. They only need to breathe the air to acquire energy and nutrition. Ghosts are very restless creatures. They indulge perpetually in either troubling others, satisfying their desires, or performing spiritual practice to obtain energy to trouble others. Their energy comes from spiritual practice. Younger ghosts tend to fear water and fire, but this soon passes when other ghosts educate them on their status." He sounded like he was reading straight from the manual. "When they do show themselves, they become a clear and vivid white, for the most part, like a white bedsheet. They can appear in all shapes and sizes. Like most ghouls, they travel by flying. Some can move faster than the wind, which is really fast. They can move right through any physical object, as if the object was not even there." Mr. Pumpkin explained their favorite pastime was to scare people. Their closest leader near here was named Gillam Ghost.

It was all so boring.

People ate three square meals per day. Or they were supposed to, anyways. I'm not sure what Ms. Pumpkin meant by square.

"Don't people eat round fruit, like apples and oranges?" I asked Peter. Again, he just ignored me.

Their sleeping habits are the same as ours. For instance, they generally tend to sleep at night time, when it is dark, just as we do. They eat all kinds of food. Of all the species, they are the most reliant on technology. Mr. Pumpkin pointed out this is their main weakness. If their technology failed somehow, they would begin to crumble as a species. Pumpkins believe that if there were no electricity or hot water available, then the human race would go extinct as a species. My goodness. That was a bold statement.

People are a social species, like us. They need each other for emotional and physical comfort. They need to interact and communicate with each other to survive.

Vampires can turn into bats. They can change the makeup of their whole body, whenever necessary. That must be really hard on their skin, I thought to myself. Mr. Pumpkin did not mention if they needed to turn into bats in order to fly. I wondered. I was sure they could fly in their vampire form. Mr. Pumpkin didn't explain why they would want to turn into a bat in the first place, though. Vampires are strong and very agile. He said that some vampires are the strongest creatures in the whole world. They drink blood. They can survive on blood, without eating any other food. They sleep during the day, then search for blood during the night. Count Dracula is their true king. All vampires report to him. But they have territorial leaders. Victor Vampire is the closest leader near us.

Werewolves are hybrids, for the most part. That means they are a combination of two different creatures. For instance, a werewolf could be made up of half human and half wolf, half human and half dog, half human and half vampire, or half vampire and half wolf. There are a multitude of different formations. They start their existence when there is a full moon. Their diet consists of eating the flesh of creatures—any creatures, dead or alive. Mr. Pumpkin said they also eat plants and flowers. Apparently they will eat anything.

Their physical make-up includes long teeth, hairy bodies, supreme strength, and a powerful sense of smell. They are addicted to blood, just like vampires. They travel by flying. Some werewolves can fly faster, depending on their formation. For example, a werewolf that is half human and half vampire would be able to fly faster than one that is half human and half wolf. This would make sense, as neither humans nor wolves can fly in the first place. Careful attention was paid to the differences between dogs and werewolves, because they can look the same. However, there are many differences between them. For instance, dogs cannot speak any English, but both species are equally dangerous to pumpkins. And werewolves can only be killed by silver bullets and other sharp silver objects.

"Tell us what happened to Walden Werewolf, Mr. Pumpkin," said Pippi. "Did he really die?"

Mr. Pumpkin didn't go into detail about his death. He said we needn't worry about that and to focus on the studies at hand. But he did confirm that he did die, and it was not known how at this time. William Werewolf was their new leader. Pumpkins were still working on getting a proper picture and biography of him. He was not one of the original favorites to succeed Walden. His rise to the top of the werewolf food chain was unexpected. Thus, he was considered an underdog.

"Is an underdog a different type of dog, Mr. Pumpkin?" asked Polo.

Witches and warlocks can only fly using their broomsticks. The closest leader is Wanda Witch. We spent a lot of study on Wanda Witch, mainly because it is known that she wants to exterminate all pumpkins. We have been told she made this declaration in her inaugural speech to the witches, when she assumed leadership. She is the only ghoul that has openly declared war on pumpkins—that we know of, anyway. This was during the aftermath of the famous War of the Broomsticks. But people prevented our extermination, as part of the peace agreement. People wanted to protect us. They were not going to allow Wanda to destroy us. People said that we were necessary and needed to be preserved.

"I met Wanda Witch!" blurted out Pashelle. Like, she's so proud of that.

Last Halloween, Pashelle met Wanda. And there was a rumor that Pashelle made a deal with her. It wasn't true. But she still met her. That's amazing. Not that I'm jealous or anything. She has mentioned it on more than one occasion, quite joyfully, I might add. Never mind that some serious calamity could have occurred. Pashelle thought she was so special because of the encounter, as if she was the chosen one or something. But in actual fact, she may never have met her. We all acknowledge that she met with witches, but who is to say it was really Wanda? So I should say that Pashelle may have met Wanda Witch.

Each module contained numerous facts and data. All of it was going to be on the final exam. It meant so much studying and memorization.

One of the experts even made noises to simulate their voices. He also gave us a demonstration of the common scare tactics used by each species. For example, lions would belt out a load roar, whereas ghosts would sneak up behind you and say boo. Witches would laugh, with a loud shriek. People could have a weapon, like a knife or a gun.

At the same time we started species study, Ms. Pumpkin also thought it was a good time for us to find a book and practice reading. Reading for fun, she called it. Not sure how reading could possibly be fun, but whatever. We were at the library one day, searching through the selection on the shelves. I examined the covers of the various books. I didn't know which one to choose, so I thought I would read the one that had the best cover picture and the one with the most pictures inside. There must have been thousands of books to choose from.

I asked Plato which one I should read. However, he seemed to be in despair.

"Ms. Pumpkin, I have read all of these books," he said. She agreed that it was not necessary for him to read any of these books a second time, and he was escorted to a different section of the library. He needed to read something more challenging.

I settled on a book called *Tales of the Ghouls*, written by Pluvi Pumpkin. It was filled with fictional short stories about make-believe ghouls. I thought it might be interesting. Pavneet found a book about exercising. Petrina found a book about the study of personality traits, written by some person doctor. Pashelle found a book about Wanda Witch. It was her autobiography. It was called *Wanda Witch: My life, in my words. Book 3*. Book 3? Like how many books does Wanda need to tell her life story? My goodness.

"Don't you think you should read book one first?" I asked.

"I have," she replied.

Oh, I thought.

Polo chose a book about a race horse named Seabiscuit.

And as soon as Ms. Pumpkin gave us the okay to take the books home, we received a scare. Well, I would say it was more of a break than a scare. The pumpkin whistles started blowing.

"Why?" we all asked. "What's going on?"

"We are having a fire drill!" she said.

"Aw!" we exclaimed.

A real live fire drill. With real live fire? No. Not real fire. Nevertheless, this was exciting. What do we do?

"Quiet, please," Ms. Pumpkin said. "Listen to the voice on the loudspeaker."

It was Mr. Pumpkin. He was announcing instructions.

"Attention. Attention. May I have your attention please? Attention. Attention. May I have your attention? This is a fire drill. I repeat. This is a fire drill. May I please have your attention? This is a fire drill." He kept repeating himself, saying the same thing over and over again, as if he enjoyed the sound of his own voice. "Please line up in an orderly manner, nearest to the closest exit, and slowly walk out of the room and out of the school building. Please follow the instructions provided by the teacher of your class."

So we all formed into a solitary line and started walking slowly and quietly out of the library, then down hallway number two and out of the main door. We were not allowed to say anything. As soon as we got outside, Ms. Pumpkin took attendance. All eleven of us were accounted for.

We moved away from the main door and watched all the other pumpkins exit the school building. This whole process did not take long at all. I would categorize it as efficient and orderly.

Then we watched the guards come rushing out of the supply center with four firehoses. We watched them attach the hoses to the fire hydrants. The water came from the dam, in Burrowsville. At first they seemed disorganized, everyone running around in different directions. But it didn't take them long to bring the hoses close to the school.

"We're ready for the water," said Mr. Pumpkin.

The water was turned on, and all four hoses started spraying water onto the school. Not the whole school, only the west wing, as that was the only part made of wood. It was a recent addition to the school building. Most of the school was brick and wouldn't catch on fire—not that I'm aware of anyway. The water was turned on only for a brief moment, and then it was turned off. The hoses were quite long and awkward to hold. Some of the pumpkins had issues holding the hoses steady when the water came rushing out. One of the groups missed hitting the school with the water altogether and instead ending up spraying the ten-year-olds, who were standing off to the side. That was ugly. Popeye felt the brunt of the spray. He got a little upset. And all by himself, in a rage, he yanked the hose right off the six pumpkins who were holding it. My goodness. We were all watching. Some of the pumpkins lost their balance and went tumbling.

"He is so strong," I remarked to Petrina.

"I know, right?"

"He must have eaten spinach," added Pashelle.

It's the strangest thing. Whenever Popeye Pumpkin eats spinach, he acquires an enormous amount of strength. It's uncanny.

"I wish I was that strong," said Polo.

"Then eat more spinach," Pashelle suggested.

"How do you know it's the spinach that makes him strong? It could be anything. He eats lots of fruit too."

Needless to say, Popeye was not happy. As he began to calm down, a few security guards went inside the school. They did a complete inspection of the whole school, while we waited and watched. After some time, Mr. Pumpkin, who acted as a fire marshal, came outside and started filling out forms.

We didn't stay in an orderly group for very long. Pavneet and Prima came over to join us.

"Are you coming later to the arena to help with the decorations?" asked Petrina.

"I don't know. They haven't given us our schedule yet. Ms. Pumpkin said we might decorate the lounge," Pavneet replied.

"But we don't know," added Prima.

"I can't help today anyway. I have to help Ms. Pumpkin with her houseguests. She's having a tea party. And I have to help her serve. And I have to go pick up her medicine from the hospital too," clarified Pavneet.

"Oh. That's too bad. She's always getting you to run errands for her," I said.

"I know, right?" said Petrina. Or Pashelle. They both like using that phrase. It can be annoying.

"Didn't you just take a whole bunch of biscuits and make house deliveries? What was that all about?"

"Because Ms. Pumpkin owed them all a favor. She wanted to send them all a gift."

"She owed them all a favor, or you did?"

"She can't walk around much, anymore. She's really old. I don't mind, anyway."

Pavneet has lived in five houses. It seems she moves every year. Last year, she was staying with pumpkins who didn't even want her there. She ended up getting sick because she inhaled rat killer spray. I know because I spent the whole night with her at the hospital.

The drill took a long time. I mean, if this was a real fire, we would all be dead by now. Like how long did we have to wait outside? It was starting to get cold.

Then we heard the pumpkin whistles. It was time to go back inside. When we got back inside, Ms. Pumpkin directed us to go to the arena to help with the Halloween decorations. The school day was over. Thank goodness.

"That was kind of fun," remarked Petrina.

Yeah, I wish we had a fire drill every day, I thought to myself. *It certainly breaks up the monotony of the school day.*

Over the next several weeks, leading up to trick or treating, we spent a considerable part of our school day learning about different species and spending time in the arena decorating for Halloween. We blew up balloons, tied them to strings, and hung them from the ceiling. We strung up banners and signs.

"What are we supposed to do with these pictures?" asked Pippi one day.

"We thought we would do something different this year," replied Ms. Pumpkin. Ms. Poppy Pumpkin was the head of the Halloween committee again this year. They were pictures and drawings off the various famous ghouls. There was a very large drawing of Wanda Witch—almost life size. The elders thought it would be a good idea if we all became familiar with their faces and physical make-up. Plus it would add a new dimension of excitement. Picasso spent much of his time sitting off to the side of the arena drawing and painting these pictures. He had lots of paper and pencils and paint. He was constantly in and out of the supply center, withdrawing these items.

It was all very hard work. And it was dangerous too. My brother Patrick was helping one day. He was left unsupervised. He wanted to climb up the ladder because he noticed that one of the banners was aslant. He can be a perfectionist at times. He climbed up the ladder when no one was helping to hold it steady. At the top of the steps, when he leaned over to fix the banner, he lost his balance. He fell. He hit the grass very hard. And the ladder tipped over and came crashing down on Penelope. She was not happy. Luckily they were both okay.

One afternoon I decided to sit next to Picasso and watch him draw. Peter and Palmer were helping him.

"What about this paint? This seems a bit different," noted Peter. They were talking about different types of paint.

"This one is different. This is washable paint. Look, I will show you," Picasso said.

Picasso then splattered the paint all over a blank sheet of paper. It was quite a mess. Then he poured some water on the sheet of paper, and the paint went away. It was like magic. The paper became soggy and wet, but no paint markings remained.

This was my chance to ask him to paint a picture for me. I told him that Petrina had this really nice painting of space and the stars and he should paint one for me too.

"Yes, Petrina loves that painting," said Peter.

"I like it too. It brings out a kind of imagination ... like anything is possible," added Palmer.

I suggested he draw me a picture of the patch. He shuffled through his plastic bag and took one out for me. He had a drawing of what looked like the downtown New Surrey City skyline. Wow. It looked great. It was exactly what I was looking for.

"You asked me about a picture like this."

"Can I have this one?" I asked.

"Pannette, I will draw you a better one. I did this a while ago. And as you can see, it's kind of worn out now," he replied. And it was. It had fold marks and dirt marks. He said he would draw me a new picture of the same, but only after Halloween. He felt compelled to finish all the pictures of the various ghouls. He was currently working on a drawing of William Werewolf. I was excited.

I wanted to change the subject. He was probably tired of conversations about drawings and paintings and pictures and colors, and whatever else. I didn't want him to think the only reason I sat down next to him was about the painting I wanted, especially since I have asked him about five times over the past year, and he still has not delivered on his promise.

"So what are you guys dressing up as this year? I want to be Cinderella," I said.

"Weren't you Cinderella last year?" observed Peter.

"Yes, I was. What about you?" I replied.

"Petrina told me to be a werewolf," Peter said.

"I want to be half werewolf, half vampire. It's called a hybrid. Hopefully I can find a costume like that," said Palmer.

Trick or treating was going to be fun. Halloween was less than a week away.

And sure enough, when we went shopping for our costumes, three nights before trick or treating, Palmer was able to find his hybrid costume. He had to collect the various clothing parts in different stores. He looked like a half werewolf, half vampire type of creature.

I dressed myself up the exact same as last year, so I really didn't even need to go to the Cambie Mall in the city to get a new costume. I had kept the one from last year in my house. Normally the used costumes are returned back to where they came after their use. It still fit. However, I still went with my friends to the city, because it can be such an adventure. Peter was a werewolf. Parson wanted to be a bat but couldn't find the proper wings, so all he wore was a bat face mask. He still looked different. Patrick wanted to be an ice hockey player. He even brought home a hockey stick but decided not to bring it with him when he went trick or treating. He thought it might be bothersome bringing so much equipment with him. Petrina dressed up as Wanda Witch. She looked scary. She brought home a broom as well—not a magic one, but a fake magic one. I'm not sure giving her a real magic broom would be such a good idea. I had to pick out Pavneet's costume. She was undecided until the last minute, just as she was last year. I helped her find a Snow White costume. Pashelle dressed up as Catwoman. I think it was because she loved the pictures of cats during species class. Polo dressed up as Batman. Pashelle and Polo forced Plato to dress up as Robin. Robin is supposed to be Batman's secretary or executive assistant. Actually I don't know what he is.

Trick or treating was fun. We were in group twenty-six. Last year, we were right at the end, and we were the last ones to return to the patch. The elders made sure this year that was not going to happen.

Peaches and Pillow were so scared and nervous when we knocked on the first door. They were both looking at me, waiting for me to take the lead. And unlike last year, we all stayed together. We all knocked on each door at the same time and said, "Trick or treat" in unison.

We came home with lots of candy—all types of candy, gum, chocolate, potato chips, juji fruit. There was so much candy in my container that I had to squish the pile downward many times, so it wouldn't overflow. I didn't want to lose any of it. There were a couple of things, though, that dampened my experience. First, it rained. There was a steady stream of raindrops falling from the sky, from the time we left the patch to the time we returned. It rained all day and night on Halloween. My Cinderella costume became soaking wet—drenched. And it came back so tattered and torn from all the running from house to house that it was not likely I could ever wear it again. And second, I underestimated the length of my feet. I didn't think they would have grown so much, but they did, because my shoes were too small. I should have tried the shoes on and tested them out for an extended period of time beforehand. But no. Not me. The shoes were just too small. My feet ached. I had a difficult time taking off the shoes from my feet. It was ugly. My big toe was swollen. I should have gotten new shoes.

The next day, we could eat as much candy as we wanted. But first, we had a Halloween party to attend to. The greatest night of the year. Lots of food, games, and fun.

We had our graduation ceremony. All of the seniors were honored. There were twenty-seven seniors this year. As each senior walked across the stage, they gave a small speech. Some of the pumpkins said the funniest things. Pavarotti Pumpkin wanted us to all sing, "Thank you, Mr. Pumpkin," not just yell it out. And he started arguing with the elders, saying that our performance was so poor and disorganized that he wanted us to sing it again. We ended up singing, "Thank you, Mr. Pumpkin" four times before the elders got fed up and ordered him off to the side of the stage. Priscilla had a six-page letter she wanted to read, but she had to skip the first five pages. I think time was the issue.

After the graduation ceremony, Pudge Pumpkin cut the Halloween cake. He is our leader. He is the elected elder one. But he was struggling. His hands were shaking. His health was deteriorating, it seemed by the day. He was spending more time in the hospital receiving treatment than ever. Someone had mentioned to me that he had been our leader for over ten years.

I ate lots of food and even more desserts and cake. I danced during our party but not for very long, mainly due to my sore feet. I spent most of the evening in the lounge, in my favorite spot, in the television room. Once I found a seat in there, I was not going to leave. I just socialized with all the pumpkins coming and going on the couches and chairs next to me, listening to their conversations. I may have even nodded off for a bit. After a while, Petrina, Pavneet, Pippi, and Pippa found me. Pavneet squished down next to me on the couch, while the other three just stood, hovering, half-dancing to the music playing in the lounge.

"How long have you been sitting here?" I was asked.

"I don't know. At least an hour. Maybe two. I was listening to everyone talking. Parker, Popeye, and Prospero were talking about how they want to sail the high seas," I replied.

"Sail the what?"

"Sail the … they want to go on a boat," I clarified.

"Pickle was asking where you were. He wanted to dance with you."

"Really? Oh. Well not now. I'm too tired. Have you been dancing this whole time?" I asked them.

"Yes. This is the best party I have ever been to," said Pippi.

"You should have seen what Pom Pom was doing. She was trying the get everyone to dance all in unison. She had these dances where we all clutched our arms, and we were all in a line, kicking out our legs."

"Yeah, and Peter kept messing it up, because he kept falling. One time, we all fell together. That was a riot."

Sounded like they were having a blast. I was just happy to get out of the rain and out of those shoes. It took me over an hour for my skin to completely dry. I don't know what it is about my skin, but it can get so water clogged.

"Where is Pashelle?" I asked Pavneet.

"She just went in line, to get our sleeping arrangements in order. Remember last year? We slept on that hospital bed."

"Yeah. I don't think I will ever forget."

Then at that instant, the music stopped playing in the lounge. And it appeared to have stopped in the arena as well. I think it's time to go to sleep. Not a bad idea.

We started to make our way back to the arena to find Pashelle. She had secured about ten sleeping spots. We got our mattresses, and blankets, made our beds, and laid down.

Peaches and Pillow wanted to sleep next to me. They ended up making my bed, because I was so tired. And they even fluffed my pillow for me. Isn't that funny? That Pillow helped me prepare for bed. I mean, I'm older than her, so it would seem logical that I would be fluffing her pillow. But she fluffed mine. I thought that was funny. It was very nice of her.

"I wonder where we put all the candy. Where is all the candy, Pannette?" she asked.

I don't know, Pillow, I was thinking to myself. And at that point, I didn't really care. I was just so happy to lie down. She also asked me why people carry small boxes called UNICEF. I didn't know the answer to that either. Pashelle, Pickle, and Penny carried the conversation for the most part. There certainly was a lot of chatter. Pumpkins are a social species. We all love to talk and tell stories. There is never any shortage of things to say.

Penny was reminding everyone about the house on Elm Street that had a makeshift cemetery in the front yard. I remembered that house. Dead bodies were rising up out of graves in the front yard. She was telling everyone that Peanut had a bad habit of cutting across the front lawns to arrive at the next house. And when she cut across this cemetery, one of the dead bodies came out of the ground and grabbed her by the ankles. Peanut freaked out. A boy named Freddie, who was handing out the candy at that house, had to put on his shoes and go outside to calm her down. Peanut was saying ...

Well, I don't know what Peanut was going to say. I didn't hear the rest of the story because as soon as my head hit the pillow, and I closed my eyes … Halloween night was over for me.

And you would think that when I awoke the next morning, I would have been one of the first, because of my early retirement. But I wasn't. Many of the makeshift beds were vacant by the time I awoke. Some pumpkins didn't even bother to sleep, I later found out.

"Hey, Petrina. Wake up," I said.

"What?" she said.

"Where is everyone?" I asked.

"I don't know. Let me sleep."

Just then Pavneet came walking over. She was up and about.

"Hey, you guys wake up. Do you know what happened last night?"

"What?"

"It's the werewolves. There are dead werewolves in the city streets," she explained.

Petrina and I got out of bed and followed Pavneet to the lounge. It was true. It was all over the news. We watched the television screens and listened to the lady give an update as to what was happening.

"The president has not yet declared a state of emergency, and it is undecided at this point what action will result. We are told a decision on that is expected soon."

"What's a state of emergency?" I heard someone ask.

No one answered. Everyone was watching and listening intently to the lady on the television.

"Fallen werewolves have been spotted as far away as Newark and Fleetwood. City officials are undergoing an investigation to determine the cause of this disaster. It's not known at this time if this is a result of a ghoul war. City council has not yet ruled this out. Plans are underway to organize a cleanup. People are encouraged to stay away from the fallen werewolves, because this could be the result of an endemic. Nothing has been ruled out. Doctors have taken some of them away to the three nearby hospitals in the surrounding areas, to undergo testing. The first werewolves were spotted shortly after most children had finished trick or treating."

Pictures were shown of the fallen werewolves. They were gory. There were hundreds of them. Their blood and guts sprawled on the city streets and splashed all over buildings and houses. Body parts had been severed from their bodies. The whole scene was ugly. It was nauseating to look at. We all stared at the televisions in astonishment. How could this have happened? Why did they all fall out of the sky and die?

"Everyone listen. Percival, can you turn off all the televisions for a moment? I want to address the situation," instructed Ms. Pumpkin. The lounge had become quiet.

"I want to assure you all that the guards have done a complete sweep of the patch, and I can report that no werewolf has fallen here. There has been no other further news to report, other than what has been reported on the news. We understand that the president has promised a full investigation. As soon as we have more information, then we will share that with you, as it becomes available. In the meantime, there is very little we can do. But we have to take precautions. Until the people have ruled out some kind of werewolf disease, and because they have fallen so close to us, all food supplies will be kept under wraps and will be apportioned only after each item has been properly inspected. This also means that none of the Halloween candy will be eaten without the proper health inspection."

"Aw!" we exclaimed.

"That's no fair."

"When do we get to eat the candy?"

"Everybody, listen to me. I know you are upset. This turn of events is very disappointing for all of us. But this is for our own good. This is for everyone's safety. Fallen werewolves are not an everyday occurrence. This is very unusual. I cannot remember anything like this happening, not in my lifetime anyways. Werewolves do not die like this. We cannot afford to have any of us become sick, if there is a widespread disease."

"But the news said it's only the werewolves. No other species is sick," noted Panda.

"Right. And ..."

"Well, then why can't we eat the candy?"

"Well, we don't know that for sure, dear. And diseases can spread. So until the people do the autopsies, and rule out disease, these rules shall be in effect."

Stupid werewolves. Dying on Halloween. So strange. They just ruined our candy eating day. Who cares if they all died? What a great Halloween it had turned out to be. Now we couldn't even eat our candy, for who knows how long.

CHAPTER 6
LESSONS

The process of food inspection was slow. Priority was given to the food we grew in the greenhouse and on the farm. The fruits and vegetables were the most important. A full two weeks passed before we were allowed to eat any Halloween candy. It seemed we were ill prepared for such a disaster. But the good news was that the disease only affected the werewolves. Or whatever it was. No pumpkin fell sick. The people counted over one hundred dead werewolves. The president did not consider the fallen werewolves to be a priority at all. And the city officials only released a white paper, which essentially declared the incident an "act of God." Whatever that meant. William Werewolf, who had only been their leader for a very short time, never issued a statement. One mass funeral was held by the werewolves. The moaning in the sky that day was loud, and it lasted the whole day. Werewolves were seen in the city streets collecting the dead. William Werewolf demanded all werewolves be returned to them, especially the ones at the hospital. People could no longer conduct the tests.

It was all that we talked about over the next several weeks—the fallen and dead werewolves.

We never did have a day where we could eat endless candy.

Meanwhile, the school lessons continued. We started technology class. We were to learn the use of computers and cell phones. We studied the Apple iPhone 5. Apparently there was a better version called the iPhone 7. Mr. Pumpkin, an expert in computer technology, was brought in as an expert instructor.

He started to give us a history lesson on mobile cellular telephones. With the first people-made phones, the user could only make a telephone call. But today, cell phones are like mini computers. He went into detail about the uses off the iPhone 1, then the iPhone 2, and so on. Yada yada yada. Like too much information, already. We decided not to order the iPhone 7, because it was not that much of an improvement over the iPhone 5. Besides, the Apple Company would have to donate those phones to us, as we don't really buy anything from people. We are forbidden to enter into a private contract with any business, as that would be a violation of the agreement we have with the governments of New Surrey City, Burrowsville, Newark, and the surrounding cities. Essentially they would need to give them to us for free. And did they? Well, apparently not. Obviously they didn't think the new version was that much of an upgrade either, because if they did, wouldn't they want us to use them?

So here we are, learning cell phones from the outdated iPhone 5. My goodness. What a calamity. And after all that, after all those tedious history lessons on cell phones and computers, we were finally going to find out what these magical devises looked like … the following week, in the next technology lesson. Well, I couldn't wait. How exciting.

And it really wasn't worth the wait. I mean, it really wasn't that big of a deal. Mr. Pumpkin showed us everything the cell phone could do, right from the basics of turning it on and off. He showed us how to access the Internet. He gave us a three-hour lesson about the importance of the Internet and its contribution to society. He showed us how to log on to these websites, where we could learn about things. We could see pictures and videos. We could listen to music. We could watch videos, like it was a television. We could read the news from the city. We could play games. Pashelle was excited to play blackjack. There were lots of things we could do on the computer and cell phone.

We learned how to use the camera to take pictures and the video to make movies. We learned about these things called apps. They are a faster, more convenient way to access a website, instead of entering this sentence or URL in the general Internet access screen. He showed us how to download them onto the cell phone. Or upload. I couldn't remember what he said, actually. But we could only download the free ones.

Mr. Pumpkin started to explain how the cell phone is a means of communication—a way for pumpkins to get in touch with people. Its proper use could be very important. It was the key to our survival, he said. That it was important for us to master text language. He gave us this manual. It was called the "Pumpkin Text Language Dictionary," or as he called it, the PTLD, for short. It was a listing of letters that translate into longer phrases and meanings. This manual was thirty-one pages. It was the PTLD version 9. Apparently, more phrases were being invented and added all the time. We had to study and memorize the manual, because of course, there was going to be a test. A text language test. Refer to the PTLD when in doubt, he said. It was invaluable.

I hoped this was going to be an open-book test, because there was no way I was going to memorize all of these texts. I started flipping through the manual, and many of them caught my eye.

AKA	Also known as
ASAP	As soon as possible
BRB	Be right back
BFF	Best friends forever
BTW	By the way
BYOB	Bring your own booze
DND	Do not disturb
DOA	Dead on arrival
EG	For example
ETA	Estimated time of arrival
ETAL	And all
ETC	And so on
FYI	For your information
GG	Good game
IDK	I don't know
IOU	I owe you
JIT	Just in time
K	Okay
KYSO	Keep your stem on
KIT	Keep in touch
LOL	Laughing out loud
LTNS	Long time no see
MIA	Missing in action
NA	Not applicable
NIS	Not in service
NP	No problem
OMG	Oh my God
OMW	On my way
OTR	Off the record
PCE	Peace on earth
PM	Private message
POL	Pumpkin out of luck

R	Are
RSVP	Reply back please
SHH	Be quiet
SRO	Standing room only
TBC	To be continued
TGIF	Thank God it's Friday
THX	Thank you
TLC	Tender love and care
TMI	Too much information
TTYL	Talk to you later
TXT	Text message
U	You
YSO	You're so orange

There were pages and pages of them. Did I mention there were thirty-one pages! There was no way I was going to memorize all of these. Like, this is TMI. This was going to be ugly. All of the tedious memorization of these letters that translate into phrases.

Why this was so important, I had no idea. As if someone could describe their true feelings by using cryptic letters as a substitute for real sentences, and hoping the other pumpkin would understand your true intention. How could the reader interpret your true meaning? I mean, LOL is lots of love. So how could anyone really understand what the sender is trying to say? That they love you or are in love with you? Wouldn't a pumpkin rather say that face-to-face? Maybe that's why we don't carry cell phones around with us. We are a social species. We need to communicate face-to-face.

We practiced sending messages and e-mails. Sometimes we were in the school library on the bigger computer that was tied to a desk with a modem and cable, and other times we were outside on the school grounds using the cell phone. We would stand outside, emailing and texting each other back and forth, using two cell phones. We did this for a few hours each day, for a few weeks. And we were all supposed to have a hands-on chance. But after all that time, and after all those lessons, I didn't get a chance to send a single text message. Not one. And no one showed me how to receive and open an e-mail or text. You can call it bad luck, I guess.

One day, when Ms. Pumpkin said it was my turn to download an app, the Internet connection was lost. It kept saying no signal. The cell phone didn't work.

On another occasion, Peter and I were to text.

"No, Peter. Learn how to text the proper way. You are supposed to use your two thumbs, not your index finger," Mr. Pumpkin instructed. "We must do this the right way, and use good habits, everyone. Please do not use any shortcuts." The elders were quite adamant about not using any shortcuts for any of our lessons.

"And I thought Peter was all thumbs. Apparently not," joked Petrina.

She can be so mean to Peter sometimes. Peter needed practice.

When it was my turn to send a text back to Peter, the battery ran out. Just when I took hold of it and was about to enter something, it stopped working. Mr. Pumpkin said the cell phone needed power. It became nonfunctional. I would characterize it as useless. He forgot to charge it. Oh, like really? And Ms. Pumpkin thought the elders were such good planners? She was always telling me to prepare and be ready. Well in this instance, I was ready, but she wasn't. My goodness.

So the two of them hurried back inside the school building to recharge it. After it was recharged, it would be as good as new.

In the meantime, we started playing with the one cell phone that was operational.

"What are you doing?" asked Polo.

"I am trying to see if there is such a thing as a pumpkin app," replied Plato.

"There's no such thing."

"What do you mean by a pumpkin app?"

"Hey, look. Here's one."

"Let's see. What does it do?"

"Do that download thing."

"Oh no, I guess not. There is one, but it's not downloadable. I guess were not allowed. It says 'this app has been blocked within your area.' Well that's too bad."

By the time the elders came back outside, technology class was over.

And there was another occasion when I wasn't able to use the cell phone when it was my turn. We were to use it to make a telephone call.

"The telephone number for this phone is 1-801-786-7546. Or you could use 1-801-PUMPKIN."

Well that makes sense. Hopefully I can remember that. You never know. One day I might need to call a pumpkin on a cell phone. I doubt that very much, though.

"The one that Peter is holding is our cell phone number two. And the number is 1-802-PUMPKIN."

"So each phone has its own number?" someone asked.

"Of course, silly. Then how would you know who was calling?" replied Petrina.

"Isn't that caller ID?"

"What's caller ID?"

What? This was starting to get confusing. TMI.

"Pay attention to Mr. Pumpkin, class. You are not going to learn if you keep interrupting," reminded Ms. Pumpkin.

Mr. Pumpkin handed me the phone. I was nervous. I was so

nervous that I accidentally dropped it. The cell phone landed in water, and that's not a good thing. It stopped working. Again. Mr. Pumpkin had to rush it into the kitchen.

"Why is he taking it into the kitchen?"

"He needs to put it in a bowl of rice, to absorb out the water," explained Ms. Pumpkin. She was not happy with me—not happy at all.

Why didn't we have more of these phones available? It was their fault. Everything was always in short supply, so it was probably not important. And if they thought it was not important, then why bother with this exercise at all?

It was no surprise that when we had the practical test a few weeks later, I failed. I mean I could have signed up to take individual training lessons, but they were held after the normal school hours. They were a part of the PTA. That stands for "Pumpkin Tutor Association." But since those were after school, I couldn't be bothered. I think I signed up for some of the cell phone lessons, but I don't think I showed up for any. I mean, why do we have to attend school after the normal hours? It seemed silly.

It was during this time that we also started our rolling lessons. And the first time I rolled, it was scary. We were at the top of the hill, getting final instructions from Ms. Pumpkin on one side, while the pumpkin engineers were conducting experiments with these great big rocks on the other side. The engineers were told to take a break. I wandered off to their side of the hill, wondering what they were trying to do. I mean, I was stressing out. I didn't want to roll. The ground was all wet, and I knew that my skin would get all soggy. And it was a long way down. I started tugging on this rope. Inexplicably, a giant rock was released, and it started rolling down the hill. I thought, *My goodness. What have I just done?* The rock rolled down the hill and eventually came to rest near a tree. It ended up trapping the engineers, who were eating lunch. They started screaming and yelling for help. I could hear them from way up top. I hoped no one was hurt. Popeye had noticed this, as he was already nearby, at the bottom of the hill. He sprinted across the field, as if he were in a race. He was going to help them. I hoped he had eaten lunch and that it was spinach. Maybe I should have gone down to help. But he didn't need my help. All by himself, he was able to move the large rock away from the tree. I saw it all unfold from atop the hill. He was able to free all of the pumpkins, sitting near the tree. Thank goodness for Popeye.

"Pannette Pumpkin. What on earth are you doing way over there? I'm fit to be tied. What am I going to do with you? You need to be over here, listening to my instruction," said Ms. Pumpkin, who had finally noticed my absence. It didn't seem she noticed the pumpkins at the bottom of the hill, though. I think that was good. And I don't think the trapped pumpkins saw what had caused the rock to come loose either.

Ms. Pumpkin walked over, grabbed my arm, and practically dragged me back to the rest of the class.

"Are you ready to roll? You better be," she warned.

She made me roll first, which disappointed Pashelle. I could see it on her face.

So there I was at the top of the hill, preparing myself to take a nasty tumble down a soggy hill. This whole exercise was silly. Why were we always learning things in school that had no purpose in real life? I mean, when do pumpkins ever roll? Never. I have never seen a pumpkin roll, or have the need to roll. School can be so silly, such a waste of time.

"Okay, Pannette. Let's go!" she barked out, while clapping her hands.

"Do it," I heard another say.

"Come on, Pannette. Go," ordered Pashelle.

Everyone was getting impatient. I tried to follow the instructions that Ms. Pumpkin had provided earlier in the day. But obviously I was not preparing myself correctly, because she was shaking her head in disagreement.

"No, Pannette. What do the instructions say? Look at the handout, and follow the steps."

I wasn't sure what I was doing. All I could do was to shrug my shoulders. I mean, I really didn't want to do this. Was this really necessary?

She became even more frustrated with me. She grabbed hold of the orange-colored manual and flipped past several pages, until she arrived at a picture of a pumpkin in the correct starting position. I quickly studied this diagram. I tucked my legs and arms to the side of my body, and I let myself fall down the hill. *Somebody please help me,* I was thinking to myself. I started twisting and turning, tumbling down the hill. I started to gain speed. I couldn't tell which way I was going after a while. It seemed I had reached warp-like speed. I was going so fast that my body ended up bouncing off the ground, and I was in the air for a good portion of the trek. I was getting dizzier by the second.

I finally came to rest at the bottom of the hill. I didn't know how long that fall took, but it was the longest time of my life. It was a relief to finally come to a full stop. And when I did, my head was still spinning. I was getting a headache. It took me quite a while to regain my balance while I laid on the ground. It couldn't have been more than five minutes before Popeye came by, helped me stand up, and escorted me to the side of the hill and out of the landing area. Thank goodness for Popeye once again. I had no balance. He had to practically carry me off to one side. At least I survived. I was still in one piece.

I was still dizzy a few minutes later, as I saw Pashelle stand up from her roll. She was walking slowly toward me. I could not believe she was walking by herself. How was that possible? She came and plopped down next to me. I mean, wasn't she dizzy?

"Wasn't that a blast?" she said excitedly. She was elated. "Come on, Pannette. Let's walk back up the hill and do the roll again," she suggested.

"Um, no, Pashelle. I think Ms. Pumpkin wants us to stay here. We need to follow instructions," I advised.

One by one, the other pumpkins in my class came rolling down the hill. Polo said it was the greatest thirty seconds of his life. Excuse me? Was he psycho or something?

"I definitely have to go on the roller coaster ride in the city."

"I know, right?"

All of us made it down the hill without incident, except Peter. As soon as he started his trek down the hill, he started to veer to the right. I mean way to the right. He was headed right for us.

"Watch out, Peter!" Petrina warned.

A few other pumpkins yelled, "Move!" They were in a sweat. They were obviously yelling out to the unsuspecting pumpkins halfway down, on the side of the hill, who were transporting fruits and vegetables. They didn't see Peter coming right for them, or surely they would have moved out of the way. Peter ended up colliding right into them. He smashed himself into the vegetable cart.

"Aw!" we exclaimed. We all saw it. It was ugly.

The fruits and vegetables started rolling down the hill, to where we were sitting. The cart went flying.

We walked up toward the accident to see if everyone was okay.

Peter had fruit splattered all over his face and body.

"Are you okay?"

"I couldn't see where I was going. Ms. Pumpkin made me take off my glasses. She didn't want them to break," he explained.

He seemed okay. Petrina and Popeye helped clean him up. One of the pumpkins workers wasn't happy. He wasn't happy at all.

"Do you know how long it takes us to transport these vegetables from the greenhouse to the school? Do you have any idea?" he asked. Peter seemed extremely guilty from the whole incident.

"He said he didn't have his glasses. He couldn't see," Ms. Pumpkin said, confirming his story, and coming to his defense. "It was his first roll, Papriko. Everything is okay. Everyone, let's help clean up this mess."

I wondered why the pumpkin workers were on this side of the hill in the first place. Why were they in the way? I mean, what were they doing? Couldn't they see him coming right at them?

We spent the next twenty minutes or so picking up the fruits and vegetables. Most of the fruit with skin was still eatable and was preserved. Only some of it had become squished and mashed under the weight of the cart.

After all the commotion had died down, Mr. Pumpkin started reading out our roll times. Polo was the fastest at twenty-six seconds. And I was the slowest at sixty-three seconds. Next time, we would all be faster, he encouraged us. Peter received an NA. That meant not applicable.

Before Mr. Pumpkin let me walk back up the hill for our second try, he took me to one side, and started to lecture me on my form and structure. He said that I had lots of room for improvement. Terrific. I mean, we have to do this again? The second time wasn't much of an improvement. I clocked in at sixty-one seconds. I wasn't the only one who had issues. Plato hurt his shoulder quite badly on his second roll. He went to the hospital for treatment of his excessive bruising. I should have gone to the hospital for treatment myself, but I was able to tough it out. It showed proof of my perseverance during this ridiculous exercise.

A few weeks later, we had our first semester exams, for all our classes. I failed all of them. Doesn't LOL mean lots of love? And I thought OMG was oh my gosh, but it's oh my God. I wasn't able to successfully load music onto the cell phone. That wasn't even my fault, as it kept giving an error, stating the memory was full. I thought vampires could travel through physical objects, but it's the ghosts that can travel through objects. I couldn't remember some of the names of the great prominent pumpkins from history class. I thought Par Pumpkin was a leader in medicine, but he wasn't. I was told afterward that he was one of the greatest golfers of our time. I got so confused. My English essay had too many grammatical errors. When I wanted to write what a pumpkin stated as speech, I ended the sentence with the double quotation, then the comma or period afterward. But it's supposed to be the other way around. It's the comma or period that comes first, followed by the end double quotation. And some parts of the essay were written in present tense, while other parts were written in past tense. Ms. Pumpkin said that gets confusing for the reader. I mean, can't pumpkins read and figure that out for themselves? Does everything have to be explained in detail? And she didn't like my topic either. I wrote about all the interesting pumpkins I have met in the lounge over the past few months. She wanted something more educational. And my fastest roll down the hill was fifty-eight seconds. We had to be under forty seconds to pass.

School was so silly. It sucked the energy right out of me. We had to write fourteen exams in three days.

I even failed cooking class. My assignment was to assist Ms. Pumpkin with a new recipe. She wanted to make gingerbread cookies. Instead of putting in three spoons of sugar, I poured in salt. I mean, they look the same. And she said to turn the oven off in seventy minutes. But afterward she claimed she said seventeen. I left them in the oven for too long. They were burnt and uneatable.

"If you had paid attention in class, then these cookies would have been fine," the head chef of the school cafeteria explained.

My school teacher and the head chef are sisters. After class, I heard them talking about me behind my back, right in front of my face. Both of them sound the same. They are very difficult to understand. They need a lesson in enunciation. They should speak more clearly.

"Perdita, are you sure you said seventeen?"

"Yes, dear, I did. Have you known me to give incorrect instructions? Besides, the instructions are written down. Here, Perlina, look. I gave these recipes to all the students."

"Did she know which bottle was sugar and which one was salt?"

"Apparently not. It's not hard to figure out, though. I have no choice but to recommend a fail. If she showed some interest, I would give her another chance. I asked her if she wanted to try again, and she said no. She said something like, 'I'm too busy.'"

Now both of them had it out for me. Okay, well maybe I was too busy. I have other things to do in life.

I mean, pumpkins make cooking seem so difficult anyway. Even when I was helping the other head chef in the dining hall with dinner later on that evening, she had eight different pots and pans going on at the same time. The meal was so complicated. I mean, whatever happened to the one-pot meal?

On the next day, Ms. Pumpkin asked me to stay after school for a few minutes. It was time for my one-on-one meeting. She suggested I take school more seriously. I was not giving my best effort. If I needed help, I should ask Peter and seek his advice and guidance. I should use him as a role model. He should be my mentor. Oh please.

That was an ugly suggestion. I mean, who wants to hang around with Peter all day? Be my mentor? What could he possibly teach me? I didn't agree with her. I felt I was doing a great job, showing enthusiasm whenever appropriate. I had only missed school eleven times due to fatigue or sickness. And I was late only sixteen times.

On the last day of class, prior to our two-week winter break, she announced the winner of the contest. I was still thinking to myself, *What contest?*

"And the winning entry belongs to … Peter! Congratulations, Peter!" Ms. Pumpkin announced.

"What does this mean?" I asked Petrina.

"It means that we're going to celebrate the New Year in the city!"

Pom Pom was so excited that she started dancing in the classroom aisle. She was waving her arms back and forth, jumping up and down. We were all excited.

Peter had a very calm and satisfied look on his face—almost like he was expecting the victory.

"So for one game, the New Surrey football team is going to use a pumpkin as their team mascot. Well done, Peter!"

Apparently, the city football team held a contest. They wanted ideas for a promotion to draw visitors to their games. Many suggestions were entered into the contest, from all types of species, including from ghouls. She proceeded to go over the ones that pumpkins entered. Pom Pom and Pashelle wanted the team to use a whole dance team, not just one pumpkin mascot. Parker suggested the team change their name to the New Surrey City Pumpkins for one game.

But it was Peter's idea for the team to use a mascot that had won. Well good for Peter.

So this meant that all of the first-year students were to attend a live game on New Year's Eve. She left us with instructions to meet back here in ten days, after our winter break.

CHAPTER 7
THE NEW YEAR

On the morning of December 31, thirty-three pumpkins, plus three teachers, headed out of the patch to visit New Surrey City. Pele, Peyton, and Parker were also invited to attend, to help chaperon. Mr. Papi Pumpkin also came, for added security, so forty pumpkins traveled that day. We left the patch through the east gate. That meant we walked through a very dark, grungy, vermin-infested tunnel, which led us to the city transit depot. From there we boarded a train that took us to a hotel. This train moved fast. We were passing by objects so fast that we couldn't even identify what some of them were. That train ride was by far the fastest I had ever traveled. When we got off the train, the New Surrey football team officials greeted us with big smiles on their faces and said, "How do you do?" They seemed happy that we arrived safely. They helped us settle into four hotel rooms. The rooms were really nice and comfortable. Very spacious. The carpet in the room was warm, dry, and soft. And the view outside the window was terrific. We saw the skyline up close. It was unlike what we experienced in the patch. There, the ground beneath us was hard and wet. And there weren't any tall buildings either.

We didn't spend very much time in the hotel room that afternoon though. The team officials waited for us to settle in quickly, and then we were to proceed to the stadium without any unnecessary delay. The stadium was walking distance from the hotel.

There were a lot of spectators in the stadium for that game. It was SRO. You see, I learned a new text. A person in the stadium announced there were over eighty thousand people watching the game. Wow! And looking up into the sky, we could see numerous witches and other ghouls flying overhead. If the announcer counted the ghouls, and us pumpkins, the attendance would have been considerably higher. It must have been an important game. One usher remarked it had playoff implications.

Just before the game started, we had to stand, and everyone sang a song. It looked like everyone knew the words, because they were singing in unison. And the roar of the crowd when the game first started was so loud that the stadium started to shake. It almost felt like an earthquake. It sent shivers through my skin.

We sat in a secluded room. It was called a box suite. It seemed like we were fortunate, because most people sat in cramped-up seats. They had to face the cold, while our suite was quite warm. There was a cold rain. We sat in comfort, with a roof over our heads. However, throughout the game, the people never cared about the cold wind and rain. I was amazed to see all of them watching and cheering. I had seen some sporting events on television, but this was the first time I had attended a live event. It seemed so important. It was the place to be. The people were overwhelmingly in favor of the New Surrey team. Many were wearing the same clothes as the players were. The usher said this was to show their support. And when their team scored, they were so elated. They were yelling and screaming at the players seemingly about every movement they made. Some of them even made very rude remarks toward the referees. Everyone seemed so involved in the game, as if their own lives depended on the outcome.

And we were seen on live television. In the middle of the stadium, there was a giant television. At halftime, the announcer made a statement.

"Ladies and gentlemen, can I please have your attention? Please direct your attention to the east side of the stadium, where for today's game, we are honoring thirty-three pumpkins. They have traveled here from the nearby pumpkin patch and are here as our special guests. They are here because Peter Pumpkin was the winner of the guest contest. It was his idea for your favorite team to feature a pumpkin as the team mascot. Please give the pumpkins a warm welcome."

Everyone started to cheer for us. We felt so special.

"Wow, Peter. You're famous now," remarked Pekka.

"Can I have your autograph?" joked Pashelle.

While the announcer was talking, our real, live activities and movements were shown on the big screen. The camera was mostly pointed at Peter. His face was projected onto the big screen. He waved to the crowd, his big eyes gleaming through his glasses. It looked like he was about to bow but decided against it. He seemed to thrive on the attention. Like brother, like sister I guess. Although I doubt if anyone could be as big a diva as Petrina. Everyone could see us. Well, not all of us. Only the pumpkins who were sitting in the first few rows could be seen on the television. I was standing in the back. I never did see myself on the television.

"They made a mistake. There are forty of us! Like, can't people count?" Pashelle screamed out.

Then a person dressed up as a pumpkin came running out onto the field and starting doing tricks. Silly tricks, I might add. He started doing summersaults and rolling exercises. He used a big pole to vault himself over another big pole and landed softly on a giant bed. Then he flung himself through a ring of fire. Like excuse me, but was he trying to imitate a pumpkin? Okay, because I don't think any pumpkin would be foolish enough to jump through a ball of fire like that. The whole act was crazy. It was embarrassing almost. I think someone from their staff should have consulted with us before implementing this weird show during the halftime of this game. None of us were sure as to the purpose of that whole exercise. People can be so stupid. I mean, don't they know how we conduct ourselves on an everyday basis? It was almost like they were making fun of us. We tried to not let it bother us. But I can tell you none of us were amused.

After the halftime show, we were provided with dinner. The food was fresh and delicious.

But our evening at the stadium ended on a sour note. Literally. As the game was coming to an end, we were provided dessert. Someone had obviously messed up. We knew the error as soon as the waitress came in with the dessert trays. The aroma was unbearable.

"Are they serving us pumpkin pie?"

"Aw!" we exclaimed.

Immediately, pumpkins started throwing up. Other pumpkins raced for the exit. Pumpkin pies for dessert! How gross! I went into the hallway to escape the odor as quickly as I could. It was an ugly scene.

The waitresses realized the error. They apologized as they quickly pulled all the trays from the suite. I don't think they really cared though. They were half snickering when they took away the trays. Another man came into the room a few minutes later, and he also apologized. He told us he would bring in a replacement menu. What was the point of that? The damage had been done. None of us wanted any dessert. He said there must have been a communication error and that he took full responsibility. Whatever that meant. Such disorganization.

The room ended up a mess. Pumpkin insides were all over the place.

"Who is going to clean this up?" asked one of the waitresses. Well not us, that's for sure. They didn't care about our health. They only cared about the mess. People can be so selfish. They were looking at us, as if we were to blame for the mess that was made. This was not our fault. Didn't the man just say that he took full responsibility?

The waitresses were so nice at first but ended up being quite rude. Even as they complained to one another about the extra work they now had to perform, one of them had the nerve to ask the other if the pumpkin pies were 50 percent off for today's game. I thought that was in bad taste. We were supposed to be their guests, but they ended up making fun of us. The whole incident left a bad taste in our mouths.

The odor lingered in the room. There was no use staying. The game was tied at that point, and they were at the two-minute warning. We didn't know who won. At that point, none of us cared.

We couldn't help but feel that people had no respect for us, whatsoever. Did any of us inform them that we don't eat pumpkin? I didn't think we had to. I mean its common sense. Such disrespect. It was a bad finish, to an otherwise exciting day.

There was a famous man in the next suite to ours, who came into our suite to ask us what had happened. He asked Peter, as the man recognized him from the big television. Peter told him about the dessert. The man had security all around him. We could tell he was important, as the security people had the same stars and badges that our elected elders wear. He also apologized for the inconvenience. He actually shook hands with Peter and congratulated him for winning the contest.

The ghouls had taken notice too. Out in the hallway, as we were leaving, we could see many bats peering through the window glass, probably wondering what was going on. I'm sure they were in shock to learn in the turn of events, as we were.

We grabbed all our stuff as quickly as we could, and we left the stadium. Petrina remarked we were leaving the stadium in bad spirits. I couldn't agree with her more.

Outside, the cold rain had turned into a light falling snow. We had to face these elements as we walked back to the hotel. I couldn't stop thinking about how our evening had ended. I didn't remember the roar of the crowd or the ambience of the stadium or the players giving their all, to please their fans. I didn't remember the tasty chicken dinner, with pasta and vegetables. Instead, all I will remember from my first live people sporting event was the ridiculous halftime show and the pumpkin pie dessert. How disappointing.

As we walked back to the hotel, we tried to forget about the incident. And we forgot quickly enough, that's for sure, because what happened next was downright terrorizing.

Just as we neared our hotel, there was a sharp lightning screech across the sky. It wasn't the usual lightning where you see a streak lasting two or three seconds, and then it vanishes. This streak lasted up to ten seconds. It was sharp and silver, and it was frozen in the sky for a long time, as if it had paused in thin air.

This may have scared a dog. Or maybe it was the sight of us pumpkins that excited the dog. Either way, there was a dog in the near distance that started to panic so much, it was able to escape from the leash tied to a pole. This was not good. An unattended dog is not a good thing for pumpkins. We braced ourselves for what might happen next. The dog was going to make a run for us. It was inevitable. The wait was excruciating. It seemed to last a lifetime, but in reality it could not have been more than a few seconds before it started to race toward us. And this was a big dog. Pumpkins yelled, "Run!"

Pashelle was the first to take off. We all followed her. We all ran away as quickly as we could. My heart was racing. I ran as fast as I could. I tried to keep up with everyone else, but I was falling behind. I didn't need to look back to know the dog was faster and was gaining ground by the second. It did not take long for the dog to catch up. He appeared right behind me in mere seconds. He was all over us. He caught up to me first because I was trailing everyone. There didn't seem to be any point in running any further. I stopped. I was scared to death.

The dog was screaming, "Ruff, ruff." The roar was loud and frightening. His big tongue was sticking out of his mouth. His teeth seemed sharper than a knife. He seemed hungry. The scene was ugly. Some pumpkins started throwing rocks and sticks toward the dog. We all wondered who the dog was going to take a leap for and bite first. I didn't want to find out. I left everyone's sight, turned a corner, and started running down an alleyway.

I was frantically looking for a place to hide. I tripped over a large round iron cover because it was loose. It was not secured to the ground. I fell over and into a hole that led to the sewer, underneath the city streets. I tried to hang onto the edge of the road up above me, but I was unsuccessful. I fell all the way to the ground. I was saved from the dog. His roars were getting further and further away. But I realized I had become trapped. I was stuck underneath the city in a sewer. How was I ever going to get out of there? Was anyone going to come back for me? Did anyone even realize that I was trapped underneath the city? I just had to be patient. I mean, someone was going to rescue me. I was sure of it.

I was surrounded by dirty water. And rats. Yes, I mean rats. I could hear their chatter. They were talking and screaming at each other, probably wondering who this visitor was. And trust me, I wasn't expecting them to serve me any tea or coffee. I was thinking they might make me their special meal of the day. It was ugly. I couldn't see them because it was dark, but I sure heard them. They were making eerie, witch like noises.

I could see the city lights up above me. I don't think I was more than six feet underground.

I started yelling, "Help!" Did any pumpkin see me fall into this hole? I was scared. Minutes passed.

I was yelling, "Help me," over and over again. I was trapped. I couldn't feel anything on the sides of the walls, something that could propel me upward, so I could climb out. The dog was long gone. All I heard were the noises of the city cars … their loud honking and engine roars.

Then luckily, after several minutes, I heard people. It looked like they were attempting to move the iron lid back to cover the hole. It may have been my last chance for escape.

"Help me!" I yelled again. They heard me. Thank goodness.

"Hello," one of them said. "Is there anyone down there?"

"Yes. It's me. My name is Pannette Pumpkin. Please help me!" I screamed.

And they did. At first, one man tried to stick out his hand, but I couldn't reach it. Then he jumped into the hole with me, picked me up, and raised me upward. The other person pulled me up, out of the hole. They saved me. If they had put that iron lid back over that hole, that may have been the end of Pannette Pumpkin as we know her.

I thanked them for their help. But now I needed to know where my friends were.

"They are just around the corner, little one," they said.

They escorted me around the corner, and I saw all the pumpkins crowded together underneath a streetlight. I heard the pumpkin whistles. When Mr. Pumpkin saw me, he came running up, grabbed my arm, and led me back to the crowd. They all greeted me with smiles and seemed relieved that I was okay.

I didn't get a chance to explain to everyone where I had been though. Many pumpkins were upset at Peter. They were asking him all sorts of questions. Why? Why were they interrogating Peter? I had missed everything that had gone on while I was trapped.

"What's going on?" I asked Pavneet.

"Where were you? We were ready to organize a search mission for you."

"I was … oh never mind. You would never believe me anyway. Where did the dog go? Why is everyone yelling at Peter? Did anyone get eaten up by the dog?"

"I don't know. A person found him and took him away."

Petrina seemed the most upset. She was quite animated. I needed to ask her what happened. It would have to be later, because we were ordered to walk quietly all the way back to the hotel. I was the last pumpkin to be accounted for. This was too much commotion for the elders. We were not in a safe position, with all the people starring at us this late at night. The elders strove for order and structure. The activities of today were far from that.

At that point I didn't care about order and structure. I just wanted to get to the hotel and take a nice bath. I smelled gross. From the sweat in the stadium, to the pumpkin pies, to the thrown pumpkin seeds, to the wet, slushy snow, to the dirty water and rats in the sewer, to the gross smell of the garbage in the city streets, all I could think of to do was to plug my nose all the way back to the hotel.

And in order for me to be first in line for a bath at the hotel room, I had to convince everyone that I was trapped in a dirty sewer.

"Smell me. I smell gross," I pleaded as we entered the hotel room.

But apparently it was those pumpkins who had thrown up who got to bathe first.

In the meantime, I laid on the hotel bed and asked Petrina why she was yelling at Peter. What did he do?

"He was talking to a werewolf. All of us were scattered all over the place. The dog ran toward the fallen werewolves."

"What?"

"There were more fallen werewolves. There were at least four of them that we counted. That's where the dog went—to go see those werewolves. And Peter was there too. And as we were running away, another one almost fell right on top of Peter. He could have been squashed. And then Peter started talking to it. What possessed him to do that, I will never know. It's so dangerous."

"What do you mean by talking? Weren't they dead?"

"They did die. But Peter said he spoke to one of them just before they died. Peter heard its last words. The werewolf said, 'Beware the lightning.'"

"What does that mean?"

"I don't know. Ms. Pumpkin thinks maybe the lightning could have killed them. They could have been struck."

"But why now?" asked Pavneet.

"What do you mean?"

"Well, isn't there always lightning? Why did the werewolves die this time?"

"Maybe they do have a disease. Lightning disease."

"What's that?"

"I don't know. I'm just saying. It seems really strange to me how all of a sudden, there was lightning, and some werewolves died. They never died before."

We talked about the stadium experience and the werewolves. After a while, I left my friends to chatter and speculate on their own, because finally, after all this time, it was my turn to take a bath. Thank goodness for that. I was starting to think that the smell and odor from the city was going to stick onto my skin. Even though the water was barely warm, I must have laid in the bathtub for over an hour. I knew my skin was going to be all soggy afterward, but I didn't care. I wanted to stay in the bathtub forever. And it was such a nice, lavish bathtub. There was plenty of leg room. And I used lots of bubble bath soap. I only came out when I heard the pumpkins say there were mere minutes before the start of the New Year. All forty pumpkins were in our room for this celebration.

The New Year can bring so much promise for the future—better times ahead for everyone. It brings the hope that all bad things will go away, with only good things to come. It's the hope that brings the excitement.

By the time I joined my friends near the television to watch the people, the pumpkins were counting down the final seconds.

Ten, nine, eight, seven, six, five, four, three, two, one. And with that, we all screamed, "Happy New Year!" Before we even had a chance to congratulate each other, we heard a loud noise outside. It was like a bomb had just exploded. Several bombs. We all looked out the window, and there were fireworks. Wow! It was unbelievable. We had all seen the fireworks celebration on television, but to witness them live and in person was something out of this world. It was magical and spectacular—and loud. It lasted twenty minutes or so. We were in awe. It was nothing compared to what we see in the patch. We only use fireworks during Halloween, and it's a very simple assortment. We normally only send one or two up to the sky at a time. And we do it mostly to scare off the ghouls. But these fireworks were on a different level. Five and six of them were going off at the same time, all exploding at various times. And it was constant. The whole event sent a surge through my body. The smoke in the sky afterward looked like there had been a great fire. It took me over an hour to calm myself down.

And then it was time for bed. The other pumpkins left our room to go to theirs.

Pumpkins were still flipping through the television channels though. I started to tire. It had been a long day. Some pumpkins didn't want the day to end. As I lay on the bed, we talked about the dog and the fallen werewolves. The caretaker was able to catch up to the dog and calm him down. He had a conversation with some pumpkins. He told them that his dog was very scared about what had happened with the werewolves and was only sensing some kind of danger. He explained how his dog was very protective of his master.

"No one cares if werewolves died."

"Yeah. Like who cares? What's the big deal?"

"And that werewolf says he got hit by lightning?"

"No. Peter claimed that the werewolf said, 'Beware the lightning.'"

"Isn't that the same thing?"

"I don't know."

"They're weird anyway. They must be. They're made up of different types of creatures."

"They must suffer from some kind of multiple personality disorder."

"Imagine being half pumpkin, half squash."

"Aw!"

"Who would want to be half squash? That would be ugly," I said.

"They would be outcasts. No one would talk to them."

"You can't outcast them just because they would be half squash. That wouldn't be socially acceptable."

"Do you know what the dog's name was? Pluto."

"What a name for a dog."

"It had such long ears."

"The man said it was a cocker spaniel."

"There's also a planet named Pluto."

"The man said his dog is normally very friendly and loves to play."

"They named a dog and a planet after me?" said Pluto.

"I don't know. I guess so."

The last thing I heard anyone say that evening was Pluto. "What a cool name for a dog," he said.

The first thing I heard the next morning was, "Wake up, Pannette. We're going to the presidential palace."

"What? When?"

"Like right now."

This was a surprise. I thought we were only going to see the game and were going back to the patch without delay. This was fine by me. The owner of the city football team was able to arrange a visit to the palace for us. I couldn't have slept for more than a few hours. The presidential palace is where the president lives. He is the leader of all the people in the land, not just in the cities of New Surrey, Burrowsville, or Newark, but all the cities, and all the people. The president is like our Grand Mr. Pumpkin.

I thought this might be exciting. It made us feel special, knowing that the president wanted to speak with us.

We all got ready as quickly as we could. It was so early in the morning that it was still dark outside. We all boarded a bus and started driving to the palace. The bus was moving fast—not as fast as the train from the day before though. The bus driver said he wanted to beat the traffic, so we were driving forty-five miles per hour. All the drivers were moving fast. But as we neared the palace, we stopped in the middle of the road. All of the cars were stopped.

"Why did we stop?" we asked the bus driver.

"Traffic," he replied.

I didn't understand. What did that mean? We said okay, like we knew what he was talking about. But none of us really knew. So we waited, sitting idly in the bus for a long time. I just listened to the normal chatter of pumpkins, constantly talking to each other, as the bus inched closer to the palace.

When we finally got to the palace, we were told the president was too busy to speak with us. He would be in meetings all day. We understood. He must have had to deal with some kind of an emergency. And he had to meet with the first lady.

"Who is the first lady? Does he mean the first ever lady on the land?" I wondered.

"No. Like, she would be dead by now," Pavneet clarified.

"People don't live forever," added Pekka.

We were still allowed to enter his big white house and look around. It was so nice, so clean, and so beautiful. We saw paintings and sculptures and art on the walls. And it was the biggest house. There were so many rooms. Each of them had their own names. There was the map room, flower room, library room, cabinet room, and briefing room. There was an arena, where they could play basketball. There were rooms named after colors like blue, green, and red. There were rooms named for the area they were in, like east, west, and north. There were so many rooms that we didn't have time to visit them all. And there were some rooms we weren't allowed to see at all—not even Ms. Pumpkin. That was due to security. I guess they were just being careful.

The best part of the whole house were the beautiful gardens. Whenever we entered these rooms, we stayed there longer. These rooms reminded us of our own home, on the patch. They were a relief almost. After all the weird and uninviting odors we had experienced in the city, these rooms were a breath of fresh air.

We ate lunch in a very large kitchen. I ate a lot of food. I was hungry. The man told us that over one thousand people could eat in this kitchen at one time. My goodness.

Then it was time to go back home. It had been quite an eventful trip.

By the time we finished our journey back to our patch, I was exhausted. That was an activity-filled two days. I barely made it through my doorway before I conked out on my bed. Patrick and Parson started asking me questions about the game and the experience in the city. I didn't provide them with many details, as I was too tired to think. I needed time to recuperate. I told them about the game and the presidential palace. I told them about the fallen werewolves. But they soon lost interest anyway, as they were too preoccupied. They had their study books open. After a short rest, I arose from my bed to glance at Patrick's textbook. It was open to a page full of graphs and pie charts. The pie charts weren't even in color, and they made for dull-looking pictures.

I heard Peaches and Pillow outside my door. I'm sure they had lots of questions also. I decided it was better to tell them about the adventure rather than to talk to my brothers anyway. Talking to Pillow and Peaches gave me a brief surge of energy. I told them everything—every little detail. I told them about how I nearly got eaten by a dog, and how I had to be rescued by people. But I didn't tell them about the werewolves. I didn't want to scare them.

Their day was nowhere near as interesting as mine. Peaches told me how she spent the whole day caring for the three older pumpkins she and Pillow live with. She did this for them, and she did that for them. I'm not even sure why they lived with them. They needed a lot of care. I don't know what the elders think sometimes. I know they must have lots of experience with child rearing, but when the young end up caring for the old, it can defeat the purpose. I mean, all three of them are really old.

Just then, Mr. Pumpkin came out of his house.

"Oh. Hello, Pannette," he said.

He provided me with a refresher on all his ailments. I had heard his story many times. He had a back ache and a neck ache. He had pain issues in his legs, even when he wasn't walking. He had trouble breathing. He was low on energy. He then started to explain his brothers' ailments and then his other brothers' ailments. Then he got confused as to which ailment belonged to which brother. I think you can add dementia to his list of ailments.

Then he started talking about something else—a completely different topic. Peaches, Pillow, and I just listened. But I lost my surge of energy. I wanted to go back inside. I wanted to go to sleep.

"Is it okay for Peaches and Pillow to sleep over?" I interrupted him.

"Oh sure. I think that would be okay. For one night."

The question and approval process was a mere formality. They had been sleeping over every other night for the past six months.

As soon as we went inside my house, I prepared for bed. I was quite sure I was going to fall asleep before the ghouls made their nightly appearance. Peaches and Pillow snuggled in next to me.

"Oh, school starts again for you, doesn't it, Pannette? I can't wait to go to school next year," said Peaches as she was eating strawberries.

Yes, it does, Peaches, I was thinking. More study, learning, and tests. All the memorization of tedious little details. Sitting in that cramped up little desk, listening to Ms. Pumpkin go on about stupid, useless topics of conversation. How fun. Just before I closed my eyes, I looked at Peaches. She seemed so excited about school. I remember thinking to myself, *Life's not always a bowl of strawberries, Peaches.*

CHAPTER 8
SPRING BREAK

The following morning, the school classes restarted. The second semester was just as boring as the first—all that ridiculous information about things I have no use for. I wondered if school for people was just as boring. It probably was. What did children learn about as they grew up?

Every two weeks, I had to meet with Ms. Pumpkin about my progress. She wanted the meetings to occur on a more regular basis. And each of these one-on-one meetings was just the same old nonsense from before. I mean, she was never happy with my work. She never smiled at me. Ever. She was always so cheerful to other pumpkins but never to me. She picked on me for no reason. It was always such a burden for her even to say hello.

"You need to try harder, Pannette. This is not acceptable. You need to start applying yourself and give more effort."

"I am trying, Ms. Pumpkin."

"Your performance needs to improve. If you need more help, then just ask."

"I have asked for help."

She was going on about my lazy habits and suggested changes

to my daily schedule. I wanted to tune her out. I mean, I had asked Peter to help me quite a few times, but he never did. He didn't care.

During math class one day, I had to solve numerous mathematical equations and needed him to provide me with the correct answers. But he didn't, despite me practically begging him. Why didn't Peter provide me with the answers? That's not helping.

There was a time when Ms. Pumpkin wanted us to research a subject and write an essay on the topic. At about the same time, Plato hurt himself during rolling class. He hurt his arm during a roll and had to spend time in the hospital. I wanted to help him get better. I wanted to help him as much as I could, so I spent a lot of time in the hospital, caring for him, and was unable to complete the assignment. The assignment was about the birth and growth of the pumpkin seed. The process of how a seed becomes a real, live pumpkin. Ms. Pumpkin thought I might be interested in that topic. And I was interested. I was to learn everything about the pumpkin seed and how pumpkins are born. She provided many books about the subject. And I studied them. I made lots of notes. I only had to compile and organize the notes into a readable document. I spent hours studying those books and taking notes. But on the evening I was to compile the notes into a proper document, I spent time with Plato in the hospital instead. I asked Peter to help complete the document on my behalf, but he refused. I don't understand why he couldn't assist me in the completion of that assignment. Why didn't he complete my assignment? He could be so selfish. I never was able to hand in my assignment, and because of Peter, I got a fail.

And whenever I asked him to clarify what Ms. Pumpkin said during class, all he said was, "Pay attention, Pannette."

One day I found myself nodding off during a class lesson. I was really sleepy that morning. I had spent the previous evening in the lounge with Panic and Perses. We were watching a game show called *Who Wants to Be a Millionaire?* They were saying that I didn't know any of the answers. They were challenging me, so I had to prove them wrong. I spent a considerable amount of time with them in the lounge that evening. When I got home, Peaches and Pillow prevented me from getting a good night's sleep. I ended up staying up really late. I was deprived of sleep. The next morning, I had issues staying awake and alert. Ms. Pumpkin was giving a history lesson about the land we live on and how the original pumpkin founders developed this land to make it liveable for all of us. It was such endless drivel. It was so boring. So during our morning break, I asked Peter what Ms. Pumpkin said. And he told me to "pay attention." Like where does he get off, being my mentor? He must be the worst role model in the whole world. What's the point of him even sitting next to me in class if he doesn't do anything to help? I found him to be completely useless. And he was supposed to be my mentor? Months went by, and despite my constant pleading, he was never any help. I was more frustrated and disappointed with Peter by the end of the second semester than ever.

I ended up failing most of my exams in the second semester also—all of them except English. I wrote an essay on life in the city. It appeared that Ms. Pumpkin agreed with everything I said about the city—the crude manners of the people, the terrible odors coming from the buildings, the garbage and mess on the streets. Don't people have any pride in their own city? I could go on and on about the things I wrote, but I won't. I failed history, math, technology, home science, and physical fitness. I tried making a video on the cell phone. I thought it was recording, but apparently it wasn't. I must have forgotten to press the red button. I probably should have checked to see if the time clock was running at the top of the screen.

Peter wouldn't help during the actual writing of these exams either. On the history exam, I wanted to get an idea of the type of answer that was required on one of the questions. So I leaned over to Peter's desk, to see if I was on the right track. And do you know what he did? Upon noticing me, he purposely put his left arm over that side of his exam paper. Like excuse me? Was he joking or what? I wasn't able to see anything he wrote.

He is the reason I failed.

The whole stress of school was such a big burden on my shoulders.

One day, a few weeks before the spring exams, the pumpkin whistles blew. It was another fire drill.

So we all followed the drill. We stood up. We got in line. And we proceeded to walk slowly out of the school. As we were coming out of the school, the pumpkin fire crew was frantically putting together the water hoses. Well at least they were working faster this time.

We smelled smoke. This time there was a real fire. My goodness. As our class exited the school building and made our way outside, we could see the west wing. There was smoke coming from that side of the school building. It was coming from one of the rooms. It was the storage room. The west wing had caught on fire. The pumpkins were spraying the building. Everyone was told to stay clear of the area. Luckily, no one was in the storage room at the time.

We all waited for the fire to be put out. The pumpkins did a great job. It was done very efficiently. The fire was put out in no time. It was a scary scene.

We overheard Penelope talk to some teachers as they passed by us.

"I saw lightning. It hit the school building, Ms. Pumpkin. It went right through that room," she explained. They continued walking and went to the office. My goodness. More lightning.

We were all told to go home. School was cancelled for the rest of the day.

The next day, it was discovered pumpkins had stolen the spring exams during all the commotion. The elders had gone to the storage room to survey the wreckage, and the exams were missing. The exams were replaced by blank sheets of paper. Some elders suggested that the fire was not caused by the lightning but instead was the work of devious pumpkins. That the fire was created only as a diversion. The main purpose of it was to steal the exams.

Penelope was explaining to every pumpkin that she saw the lightning. Peter claimed the same thing. But I thought it strange that just before the whistles blew, Peter suddenly left the classroom. He claimed he had to use the toilet. Was that even true? I mean, maybe that's why he got such good marks in school all the time. He was able to preview the exams. Because he didn't look very smart. He could barely see through those thick glasses of his.

We recalled that Peter and Panic had a heated conversation as they left the school grounds the previous day.

Petrina started to walk with Peter. We all did. She was in his ear as we walked toward the lounge after the fire had been put out.

"I didn't steal the exams," claimed Peter.

"Then who did? Was it Panic?" asked Petrina.

"No. I don't know. Maybe no one stole the exams. It's possible that—"

"You heard Ms. Pumpkin. The exams are gone. How do you think that happened? By magic?" said Petrina. She was insistent.

My mind started to wander again. New exams would have to be created. Who would steal the exams? Peter thought no one stole them. Why? Because that's what he would say if he did steal them, no doubt. Wasn't he with Panic earlier? Because that is something Panic would do.

So the elders started questioning all of us—not just Peter, but all of us. Including me. As if I would do something like this? I have never stolen anything in my life. Never. Well, maybe that's not 100 percent true. I have stolen a few things from time to time. Last year, I stole some medicine from the hospital. But that was to help Pavneet. She was sick at the time.

"Where were you, Pannette, at exactly one forty-five on that day?" an elected elder asked.

"I was in class."

"Tell me what you were doing at the time."

"I was listening to Ms. Pumpkin."

"Good. What was she saying?"

"I don't know. I cannot recall."

"Then how do we know you were in class?"

They were such ridiculous questions. The elders wanted those exams back. They pleaded with me. They gave me a lecture on the morals of being honest.

The elders began to conduct surprise inspections on a more regular basis. Every home was searched. This went on for the rest of the semester.

"My home has been searched two times. They went through all of my personal belongings," complained Pashelle.

"So. My home has been searched four times in one week!" responded Panic.

"That's because you probably stole the exams. You stupid goof!"

So they had to prepare new exams. And I had studied so hard to prepare for the original exams. I studied day and night, constantly thinking about them. I mean, I know they were surprise questions and exams are not open book. But even still. The thought of it created an unnecessary anxiety. I became all discombobulated. And the accusations and innuendos created stress and grief. It was no wonder I failed. I was unable to concentrate properly.

Oh well. I couldn't be worried about that now. It was spring break. The second semester was over. It was now two weeks of rest and relaxation. I could relax in the lounge and take part in idle chatter with my friends. I could do the things that give me the most pleasure in life. I mean, we only live once, right?

However the rest and relaxation soon disappeared. I was in the lounge with my friends. Petrina, Pavneet, Plato, and Polo and I were just chilling, when Pashelle suggested we sign up for golf. My goodness. I didn't want to take part in that nonsense.

"Are we going to sign up for golf?" she asked.

"Yes. That's exciting!"

"What for?" I questioned.

"It could be fun. I don't know. It's something for us to do."

"I'm going to sign up," said Polo.

"Same with me," confirmed Pavneet.

"It would be fun,"

"Good. Let's do it."

Great. Now everyone wanted to play golf.

"The first lesson starts tomorrow, so we should probably go sign up now. Come on everybody."

Like now? Pashelle wanted to sign up now? It was raining. At least I convinced everyone to wait a day, to see if they would change their minds. But they were steadfast. When we met up in the lounge the next morning, and before we even had a chance to sit down or have breakfast, we set out toward the golf course. The practice qualification rounds were starting. If a pumpkin wanted to be a part of the next qualification round, we had to score well enough by playing the full eighteen holes under a certain score.

I was handed four different types of golf clubs, and without any practice, I was told to go to the first golf hole, or to the first tee, as Mr. Pumpkin called it. Pepper was my playing partner. That meant he counted every shot that I took, and I was to count every shot he took. We watched Plato and Polo hit their balls off the first tee. Then after a few minutes, Mr. Pumpkin said it was my turn. Well my first practice round did not start well. Right away, Pepper told me I was using the wrong stick. I was only to use the putter on the grass that is more evenly cut, when my ball was really close to the hole. I was to use an iron off the first tee. I'm not sure it would have made a difference because it took me four swings off the golf club before I even hit the ball. And when I did make contact, the golf ball just rolled off to one side, into the bushes. It ended up trapped behind a big bush. And then Pepper penalized me two points because I picked up the ball and moved it out of the bushes. I mean, I only did so to make my second shot easier.

"Never touch the golf ball with your hands without the permission of the scorekeeper," Pepper told me. My goodness. More rules.

It took us almost three hours to finish the round. On the seventh hole, we had to let Pashelle and Pavneet play ahead of us. By the thirteenth hole, we had to let Prime and Panic pass.

"This is really embarrassing," I heard Pepper murmur to himself.

Needless to say, I failed. I should have stood on the other side of the ball, like Pepper. He was a lefty, as he called himself. He performed much better than I did. However, he failed too. And he started blaming me for his failure. On the ninth hole, I saw his ball coming down the hill, near Star River. I mean, I was standing close by. Nobody was looking. I wanted to help him. So I stretched out my foot to stop the ball, to see if I could save it from rolling further down the hill and into the river. But I ended up deflecting the ball, and it caught the steeper part of the hill. It ended up rolling down the hill even faster. The golf ball ended up in Star River anyway. I got a bruise on my foot for my efforts. I was a little clumsy, not to bring the ball to a complete halt. It cost him two points. He was pretty mad at me.

"I was just trying to help." I tried to defend myself.

"You're not supposed to touch the ball with any part of your body. Not mine, not yours. Not anyone's. That was a good shot, Pannette. It was going right where I wanted it to go. If it had stopped right there, as it was going to do, then I had a great angle for my second shot. You can't do that. There is no cheating in golf."

"I wasn't trying to cheat. I was just trying to help you," I said to him. I mean, get a life. It's only golf.

But that was an unfortunate bit of bad luck for him because he failed by two points. He had to come back the next day and attempt to qualify again.

I met my friends at the clubhouse after the round. Pavneet was the only one of us who passed and admitted into the qualifying tournament. The rest of my friends wanted to come back the next day. I was not sure if I wanted to. I was all sweaty. It may have been the hottest day of the year up to that point. It had been raining every day, seemingly. But that day was nice. I don't think I was quite used to the heat yet.

After playing golf, we decided to get a late lunch, early dinner. As we were about to cross the Water Gate Bridge, we ran into Pol, Pod, and Peter. Actually, those are only their nicknames. Pol is short for Polaroid, and Pod is short for Podrick. It's difficult to say Polaroid, so we just say Pol. And since those two always hang out together, we just refer to them as Pol and Pod. In actual fact, we say Mr. Pumpkin now, because they are elders. They were practicing on the cell phone, taking pictures.

"Mr. Pumpkin, take our picture," said Pashelle.

"Okay, sure. Why don't you all line up? Why don't you go in the picture too, Peter? Stand next to your sister. Actually, move over this way, so we get the school building in the background," instructed Mr. Pumpkin.

"This is going to be cool."

"It's like we're all models, posing for a fashion magazine."

"Yeah. Like famous pumpkins."

"I know, right?"

So there we were, standing on a grass field near Star River, and Mr. Pumpkin was getting ready to take our picture. I was at the left, standing. Peter was next to me, then Petrina. Plato was to the far right off me. Pavneet, Pashelle, and Polo decided to sit down. But just as Mr. Pumpkin readied himself, my bow came untied, probably due to all the sweat on my stem from playing golf. I put my hands up to retie my bow, and cried, "Wait!" But he didn't wait. He took the picture.

"What a nice picture this is going to be," claimed Petrina.

"You have to get a print out and give us a copy."

"No. Wait. Take another one. Please," I begged.

However, my plea came too late, as everyone had already broken formation and scattered. My goodness. This was no good. I didn't think that picture is going to turn out very well for me. I sure hoped that picture wouldn't get printed or posted anywhere. Plato had talked about creating a pumpkin app and thought it would be great if that picture could be posted on that app. I sure hoped not. I wished that picture went nowhere.

The next day while we were in the lounge, I tried to convince my friends not to try out for golf again.

"If you really don't want to play, then why don't you come with me to the greenhouse?" offered Peaches.

"What's happening at the greenhouse?" I inquired.

"The new baby pumpkins are there now."

"They're probably only seeds, Peaches. They are not pumpkins yet."

"I know. But it's still fun to watch them."

"You mean watch seeds grow? That's like watching paint dry," I advised.

"I'll come with you," said Pavneet.

So we all left the lounge that morning and headed west through the gardens of the eye. The flowers were blooming. The eye looks so much prettier and beautiful in the summer because of the flowers. Especially the rose garden. The pumpkin gardeners grow pink, red, and white roses. The pink ones are my favorite.

So while most of us went into the clubhouse to check in and start our round of golf, Pavneet and Peaches went further south to the greenhouse.

"Beware the fallen werewolves," said Pashelle.

"Why?"

"I don't know. I heard someone say that to me the other day. I think it's supposed to be a joke. So I'm just saying. Watch your back … And your heads."

We started golfing. I was paired with Petrina this time. It really bothered me that she was doing better than I. She was putting the ball in the hole in five shots, sometimes four. I don't think I put the ball in the hole in less than six shots on any of the eighteen holes. We both failed. Golf can be such a frustrating game. It requires a great deal of patience and concentration and lots and lots of practice.

I was at the scorers' table, handing in my scorecard when Peter asked how I did.

"Not too well. I hit the ball into Star River six times."

"That doesn't help."

"No, it doesn't. Did you play? How did you do?"

"I made it. I qualified."

"Focus on your mechanics, Pannette. Keep your head down. Don't look up to see where your ball went until you have actually hit it," suggested Mr. Pumpkin.

I mention this day of golfing because just as we handed in our scorecards, the strangest thing happened. Lightning had struck and on a clear, sunny day, no less.

"Aw!" we exclaimed. All the pumpkins in the clubhouse saw the lightning. How was this possible? It was not even raining. And sure enough, Pashelle was right. We saw three werewolves fall down from the sky. They landed off in the distance in Burrowsville. We could hear the shrieks from the sky. They were loud noises. They didn't sound like werewolves falling from the sky. They almost sounded like witches. The whole incident was weird. Peter agreed with me that the noises sounded like witches.

"What's going on, Mr. Pumpkin? Why are all the werewolves falling? Isn't it a full moon today? We were told in species class that werewolves are born on a full moon. They don't die," said my brother Patrick. I didn't even notice he was standing next to me.

"How do you know it's a full moon?"

"Maybe the werewolves do have a disease."

"They might not be werewolves."

"Let's go see them."

"No way. Too dangerous."

"Are you scared?"

"There's probably blood everywhere."

"I know, right?"

"Was that really lightning?"

"Maybe it was a meteor."

"What's that?"

"Maybe the aliens are killing them."

"There's no such thing as aliens."

"How do you know?"

"Don't you think there is life on other planets?"

"Are the aliens invading, Mr. Pumpkin?"

"How come there were no UFOs then?"

"Maybe they are invisible."

"Are UFOs invisible, Mr. Pumpkin?"

As we were discussing the werewolves, we noticed the pumpkin medical staff racing toward us. They were carrying a makeshift bed.

"It's fine, Doctor. We are all fine. Is everyone here okay?" asked Mr. Pumpkin.

"I think so."

But the medical staff did not stop for us. They raced onward, further south. They were headed toward the greenhouse. We all wondered what could have happened there, so we all followed the medical staff.

Once we entered the greenhouse, we found Pavneet lying down. She wasn't moving.

"What happened? Did any of you see what happened?"

My goodness. What was wrong with Pavneet? Why wasn't she moving?

"Everyone back away. She needs space. Did you see what happened, Parse?" asked Dr. Pumpkin.

"No. I didn't. I was outside. Peaches told me that Pavneet fell down, so I came running inside. That's when I called you, Doctor. I really don't know what happened."

I could see that Peaches was in half shock and couldn't speak. All the gardeners were outside and only came inside when Peaches called them. Nobody had seen what happened to Pavneet. She laid motionless on the ground. This was really scary. Dr. Pumpkin opened her eyes, so he could shine a tiny flashlight inside.

"Okay. Let's get her on the bed and get her to the hospital," he ordered.

The medical staff put her on the bed and slowly carried her back to the hospital. They were being very careful. It took them a long time to return to the hospital. When they went inside, we were all told to stay outside. Many pumpkins had gathered there, and we all wondered what had happened.

The whole incident was strange. The lightning on a clear sky. There was no rain. There were hardly any clouds in the sky.

"Do you think she got hit by the lightning?" someone asked.

Peaches was still in shock. It would appear she was the only one who may have witnessed the event. I mean, this was really scary. What if she got hit by the lightning?

We all feared the worst. We spent the rest of the day outside the hospital. We were not allowed inside. By nighttime, her condition still hadn't changed. We were told to go home. Her condition hadn't changed the next morning either. We actually didn't even know what her condition was. The doctors, nurses, and medical staff still hadn't passed on any news.

Days had passed, and still no news or statement was issued regarding her condition. Peaches had finally collected her thoughts after three days. She finally gave her account as to what had happened. And she didn't see what happened. She was watching the gardeners outside. Then the lightning came. She saw the lightning just like we all did. She saw at least five werewolves fall from the sky from her vantage point. She was looking westward. She heard a heavy, dull sound from inside. She went to see what happened and found Pavneet lying on the floor, facedown. Then she ran back outside to the elders and told them that Pavneet fell down and wasn't moving. The elders phoned the hospital.

The whole situation was very serious. We were all scared. It seemed that our lives had stopped.

After four long and gruelling, sleepless nights, Dr. Pumpkin finally announced that Pavneet had awoken and would make a full recovery. She was okay. Thank goodness. We were all so worried.

We were told she was not hit by the lightning after all. A complete test was done on her body. Peaches was also okay. She only stayed one night in the hospital.

A full week had passed before we were allowed to visit Pavneet. She had bandages wrapped around her head. Other than that, she seemed in good spirits. She explained the event.

"I was just looking at the pumpkin seeds. A few elders were inside. A few elders were outside. Peaches and I were actually getting ready to go back. No … no elders were inside. I don't know. I don't remember. My head still kind of hurts. We were going to see if any of you guys qualified for the golf tournament. So Peaches went to tell the elders we were leaving. And then the strangest thing happened. There was lightning. Did you guys see lightning strike? It came right through the greenhouse roof. I saw real live electricity, right in front of me. I don't know how else to describe it. It was a ray of real sharp silver light, with smoke coming out of it. I was stunned. I was taken aback. I must have stepped backward, because I think I hit my head against the wall behind me. That's all I remember."

"The doctor said you may have suffered a concussion. They did tests. You didn't get hit by any of that electricity."

"I know. They told me. I was pretty lucky. I mean, I saw it come right through the roof of the greenhouse. It was like in slow motion. It was like it stayed in front of me for like five seconds. This ray of light. It was frightening."

"You scared us."

We weren't allowed to visit Pavneet for very long. We could only visit for twenty minutes per day for the next week.

I stayed in the hospital all the time during spring break though. I was helping the nurses care for the other pumpkins in the hospital. I changed bedsheets. I talked to the sick pumpkins. I ran errands for them. I felt so useful. I felt so important. When pumpkins needed assistance, I was there to help them.

Pimi was in the hospital one day because she had issues adjusting to the heat after a long cold winter. She was dehydrated all the time. I kept an eye on her, making sure she had enough water to drink. Ms. Pumpkin was in the hospital one day because she fell down and twisted her ankle. She couldn't put any weight on her foot. Each day, I helped the nurse take her for walks until she was able to walk by herself.

It was such a joy watching pumpkins improve. And I felt so proud, knowing that I helped them.

I watched the doctors take examinations of pumpkins and conduct tests. I observed the instruments they used and watched them work. They were so focused and very methodical. They paid so much attention to detail, double and triple checking each test result.

Each day for the next week, not only did I spend time with Pavneet, but I was helping every pumpkin in the hospital.

The medical staff, however, kept telling me to go home. They said that since I was not properly trained, I shouldn't be assisting them. It seemed they viewed me as someone who was just in the way. It was almost like they didn't want me to help—that I was an additional burden for them. They made me feel guilty for trying to help them.

During this time, Peter was visibly upset. He had become very emotional from the incident. Some of us were thinking that maybe tests should have been done on him too. He was acting so strange. Normally he was very calm and collected. Petrina was saying how he was in and out of the office, talking to the elected elders. She didn't know why. Peter wouldn't tell her. He wouldn't tell any of us. I saw him talk to the medical staff many times. One morning he was arguing with Dr. Pumpkin. He was almost yelling at all the doctors, telling them to act. "We need to act now, before it's too late," I heard him say. Too late for what? It was already discovered that Pavneet and Peaches were fine. Whenever we asked him, he wouldn't tell us what the issue was, though. He completely ignored us. He could be so mysterious. He was even ordered not to visit with Pavneet when she was awake. The medical staff didn't think it was a good idea. It would only upset her. Petrina didn't think it would be a good idea either. After all, Petrina knew him best. I always thought Peter was kind of strange, always keeping to himself and never really sharing his feelings with anyone.

I asked Dr. Pumpkin, "Why is Peter so upset with you?"

"He is not upset. He wants us to test the pumpkin seeds to ensure they are okay. And that is what we have been doing. He was able to convince us to do the tests. It can be very dangerous to their health, because we have to dig the seeds out of the ground. Digging them out could cause permanent damage to them. We were reluctant at first. But we are testing three of the seeds now."

"Oh. Since they were so close to the lightning?"

"Yes."

"And are they?"

"I cannot talk about that with you, Pannette. You shouldn't even be here in the hospital."

"Pavneet seems to be getting better. She is starting to remember things again. Is that what a concussion means?"

"Yes. The brain doesn't function properly when you suffer a concussion. She had a loss of memory. She has been diagnosed with a case of amnesia. It can be very serious."

"I want to care for pumpkins when I grow up. Do you think I could volunteer in the hospital?"

"Only the brightest and smartest pumpkins can be in the hospital all the time. This work requires a pumpkin to be very responsible and mature. The pumpkin has to prove to us that they belong here. We cannot have any doubt about them. It requires years and years of dedication and continual study. We normally only select the pumpkins with the best exam scores during school."

I tried to show him that I belonged in the hospital. I would provide him with my prognosis on Pavneet. I would ask Pavneet about significant events in her childhood. And she made progress every day. I tried to be as honest as I could with my evaluation. After a while, she was able to recall most of the things I asked.

After it became clear that Pavneet would make a full recovery, she was released from the hospital. She was told to stay at home for an additional two weeks. But she didn't. When she was released, she was back at school. Spring break was over.

CHAPTER 9
FIELD TRIP

By the time school restarted, Peter had settled down. He seemed satisfied with the medical staff at the hospital. He was sadder and more glum than normal, but he wasn't so upset with the elected elders anymore. Actually many of the elders seemed a bit sad, when school re started. We all had noticed this. Peter was still spending a lot of time at the office talking to some of the elected elders, Petrina had noted. Not all of them though, as Pudge and Ms. Patricia Pumpkin refused to meet with him. The only thing we thought was that something terrible happened to the pumpkin seeds. But this was only speculation on our part because no official announcement had been made about them.

Peter didn't want to come with us on our field trip either, but he had no choice. Participation was mandatory.

I was actually very excited about our field trip. I was relieved that Pavneet had made a full recovery. She needed an outing to cheer her up. We all did. We were going to Burrowsville to visit the water park and zoo. I was adamant that I was going to enjoy this outing. I was certain that for at least one day, I was going to enjoy school.

That morning, we had to arrive at school two hours prior to the usual time for preparation. We walked to the greenhouse and then through the very thick, dense trees on the west side of the patch. We refer to this entrance to Burrowsville as the farm exit. Once on the other side of the trees, we waited by the side of Linden Road for a bus to emerge. When one arrived, we boarded. Then we waited for twenty minutes or so, sitting in the bus, while the bus driver was standing outside. What was he waiting for? I thought we should have left without any further delay. I was excited to visit with all of the animals.

Then from behind us, we saw more pumpkins appear. And they boarded another bus that parked ahead of us.

"Why are they getting on that bus?" asked Pashelle.

They were the eight-year-olds. She was obviously referring to Portia, Paige, and Paris. Pashelle has had many disagreements with them over the years. Pashelle thinks Portia is too pushy and arrogant. And she is. But I have never had a problem with her or her friends.

"Are they coming with us? Why?" she asked Ms. Pumpkin.

She seemed perturbed. I'm not sure why. Just let it go, Pashelle, I felt like telling her. I mean they're allowed to come too. Let's just have fun.

The bus ride was about fifteen minutes. Apart from the dense line of trees, Burrowsville is mostly farm land. We rode the bus right to the edge of Burnaby Bay. We were greeted by a tour guide when we got off the bus.

The park was so big. There were so many animals. And there were so many people there as well. The tour guide said it would take us all day to fully embrace what the park had to offer.

Once we entered the zoo grounds, the first animals we met were lions, leopards, and tigers. They were all in cages. And it was a good thing they were in cages, because none of them seemed very friendly. None of them smiled at us. As we approached the cages, they awoke from their slumber and made their way to the edge of the bars, to where we were standing. I was amazed at their size. They seemed really strong. Their mouths were so big. And their teeth seemed so sharp. And I thought that dogs had sharp teeth.

"Do these animals perform in the circus, Mister?" asked Petrina.

"You can call me Mr. J if you like. Well, some of them do. Not all of them. They have to be tamed first," he said. "It takes years and years for us to tame them. Then they go to the circus for the full training."

When we arrived at the next set of cages, none of the animals responded to our presence. They were tigers. They all laid quietly.

"What's wrong with them? How come they're not moving around?"

Parker joked they must have done too much partying the previous night. That was kind of funny. Mr. J said they were feeling sick. They were doing tests, but the results hadn't come back from the hospital yet. They weren't exactly sure why they had been so quiet. They had been in this idle state for quite some time now.

"They are probably doing a cat scan. I learned about that in the hospital," Pavneet whispered in my ear.

"Why do you think they are sick, Mr. J?"

"Well, the strangest thing happened. A werewolf fell down from the sky last month. And he fell right into that cage. Those tigers ate the werewolf. They ate every last piece of him. Even the bones. Now, normally tigers don't eat werewolf ... so that may be the cause. Werewolf is a different type of meat. We actually monitor all the animals' diets quite regularly. The werewolf falling in there was unusual and unexpected. Before we had time to retrieve it, he was already eaten right up. We think that type of meat could be the cause of their sickness, but we really don't know. The tests are ongoing."

"Did any other ghouls fall from the sky, Mr. J?"

"It looked like that crazy witch was going to fall in there too. But she didn't. She just flew down to have a look at the dead werewolf. Actually I wasn't there. One of the other zookeepers was telling me all of this. He was saying that the witch made a comment. The witch said something like, 'Bye bye, wolfie.' Then she left the scene."

"Which one? Was it Wanda?"

"I don't know. The zookeeper said it was the one with the fancy broomstick and the loud shriek."

As we moved through the zoo grounds, the tour guide gave us a brief description of each animal and why the animal was so special. He said that cheetahs are some of the fastest animals on the planet.

As we were visiting with the bears, Panic threw bits of popcorn into the cage. We weren't supposed to do that. We weren't supposed to alarm them in any way. One of the bears jumped up and leapt toward the bars of the cage. That really scared us. He gave us a loud growl. Mr. J was not happy with Panic. Neither was Mr. Pumpkin.

"Listen, if you are not going to behave, then we are going to cancel this outing, and we are going back home!" warned Mr. Pumpkin.

"Don't be stupid, Panic!" yelled Pashelle. "Do you really have to ruin this for everyone?"

There were so many of us pumpkins that I hardly ever got a chance to get up close to the cages. When we moved to a new cage, everyone surged forward. The eight-year-olds always seemed to be one step ahead of us. And there were a lot of people inside the zoo also. They were a part of the tour. People can be so pushy. I mean, it was like a jungle in there.

We moved to the cages that housed apes and gorillas.

"Do people come from apes?" asked Paige. One person overheard the question, and he angrily said no. The person said that was a ridiculous notion. None of us believed him though. I mean people and apes look so much alike. Except for the females. They seemed to have less hair on their bodies compared to the male people and the apes.

We all had so many questions. Mr. J could not keep up with us. All of us were so fascinated, and we were talking a mile a minute. We were all so amazed at these animals.

We visited different types of birds. We saw birds called parrots that spoke English. They liked to repeat the things we said. No other animal spoke English—not even the tamed ones that perform in the circus. And none of the apes spoke. They just growled. We met with pelicans and peacocks. And we met this real beautiful bird called the pink flamingo. It looked so pretty.

We didn't visit with any eagles though. That was a bit of a disappointment for me.

"Excuse me Mr. J. If people originate from apes, then why don't they speak English?"

He was not able to answer many of the questions we had. Mr. J wasn't so smart.

He asked us if we wanted to go to the farm, where there were pigs, chickens, roosters, and hens. But we said no. We actually saw those animals in the patch, on our farm.

Polo expressed his disappointment that there were no horses in the zoo.

After visiting with the animals, Mr. J led us to a private lab. He said that his team was working on recreating a new type of animal. Actually it wasn't new. It was an animal that used to live on the land but didn't anymore. He showed us these giant eggs. The animals were still inside the eggs. He said they weren't ready to come out of the shells just yet.

"Where will they live?"

"Oh not here."

"Will they live in the cages, or will they live out in the wild?"

He said he wasn't sure. It was very possible they would need to build a brand new park, just for these creatures. This species would be much stronger, bigger, and faster than any species that anyone has ever seen. Everyone would be so fascinated by them that the park would make lots of money. His team was trying to replicate a species that ruled the land many years ago.

"People are going to give an arm and a leg to see these things," he muttered to himself. He seemed really excited about the project.

Then he led us into a souvenir shop. Each pumpkin was allowed one souvenir. I didn't find anything I liked. Neither did Petrina. We decided to wait and keep searching for something better. Polo got a stuffed tiger. Plato got a book about apes. Pashelle noticed that Picasso picked out a coloring book with lots of pictures, so she got the same thing.

Then we left the animal zoo. Mr. J said good-bye to us. We now had a new tour guide. She introduced herself. Her name was Heidi. She first took us underground. We saw various types of fish in small glass tanks. Then we went into another room, where we actually got to see out into Burnaby Bay. We saw bigger fish swimming around, and some of them looked so pretty. Apparently we could see octopus, but none of them surfaced. The lobsters, crabs, and starfish weren't visible either, so that was kind of boring.

Just as we were to go upstairs, a family of mermaids swam by and waved to Heidi. Heidi waved back. I think they knew each other.

"What is her name, Heidi?"

"Her name is Molly Mermaid, and that's her family. It looks like they are getting ready to have lunch," she explained.

"What type of species is Molly? Is she a fish or a person?"

"Mermaids are hybrids, sweetie," she answered with a smile.

Then it was time go back upstairs, and we were going to watch a dolphin show. We were sitting in a small arena, waiting for the dolphins to appear. Then Heidi said the weirdest thing. She asked us if we were hungry and if we wanted to eat lunch. She asked if we wanted hot dogs. Well pumpkins don't really eat dog. Pumpkins have never eaten that species. Not that I know of anyway. Our meat is usually restricted to chickens and pigs that we grow on the patch, or fish. And we eat lots of fruits and vegetables. The fish actually were brought in from around here. We were told the fish market was close by.

When Heidi left our view for a brief moment, Piper provided more detail about hot dogs.

"It's not really dog," she said.

"What is it? Beef? Pork? Chicken?"

"Is it a combination of meat?"

"It's mystery meat. No one really knows. But it's not dog."

I hope not. I thought dog was man's best friend. It would be strange if they ate them.

"Pavneet, you seem so much better now. How is you head?"

"I had this big bruise over here. But the swelling has come down. And I'm not getting any more headaches. Well, I did a little today. Those lions were loud, weren't they?"

"I know, right?"

"I got a headache listening to them."

"So you didn't get hit by the lightning?"

"No. I don't think so. The lightning was kind of in front of me."

"How?"

"It came right through the greenhouse roof."

"No. I mean how? It wasn't even raining."

"And those werewolves keep dying. Did anyone hear the noises when they were coming down?"

"They didn't even sound like werewolves."

"They almost sounded like witches."

"You know, I think the witches were watching. They were probably elated. You know how witches can be."

"I thought I saw Wanda."

"What?" Peter asked.

"I said I thought I saw Wanda Witch. She has the loudest shriek. Her voice is so recognizable. It was like she was laughing."

"She must be really happy. All this time, we have been told that werewolves are born on full moons. But they died instead."

"Isn't it strange how the lightning came, and there was no rain? There were hardly any clouds. There was no thunder afterward. How is this all possible?"

Just then the announcer started talking over the microphone. She welcomed the trainers. There were two of them. Then the announcer introduced the three dolphins, who jumped out of the water. Their names were Dana, Daphne, and Drake. Drake was the male. The others were female. Daphne was the baby dolphin. First they did some warm-up exercises. They jumped up and down, in and out of the water. The trainers told them to do things, and they did. They jumped through plastic rings, similar to what the pumpkin mascot did at the city stadium, but there was no fire. They performed all types of tricks. They did flips and summersaults when they were in the air. Sometimes they did things by themselves, one at a time. Other times, they did things in unison. And each time they did something, the trainers would give them food as a reward. It was a great show. They were very entertaining.

After observing all these animals up close, I wondered what life would be like them. I mean, sometimes I would think what life would be if I was a person, with their long arms and long legs and living in that filthy place. That would be strange. But to think I would be a lion, a bear, or a bird—well, that would be totally insane. I'm sure glad I was born a pumpkin.

After the dolphin show, we were invited into another souvenir shop. But again Petrina and I didn't find anything we liked. We hoped there would be more shops somewhere else. Pavneet got a very large stuffed dolphin. It was so large that she was having difficulty grasping and taking a hold of it. It was larger than her. We left the zoo. But since we still had time in our day, we went to visit the fish market. We ate lunch at a fish restaurant. I ate salmon and potatoes. It was the best salmon I had ever tasted. It was so fresh. I wanted more. And the potatoes had butter and sour cream. Plus we made sure there were lots of vegetables. It was a terrific tasty lunch.

The restaurant was right near the beach. It was really nice outside. We sat on an outdoor patio. Many of us wanted to play on the beach, so we all went to the beach. The sand beneath our feet felt so warm. The eight-year-olds came prepared. They had obviously been here before. They brought out a volleyball net, and many pumpkins played volleyball. Some pumpkins played beach soccer. Other pumpkins started building sandcastles. Some of them were a little messy. We watched Picasso construct a beautiful castle, similar in shape to the big white house where the president lived.

Petrina wanted to get closer to the water, so the two of us held hands, slowly inched our way closer to the beach shore, and positioned our feet on the edge of the water. We took baby steps out in the water and stopped when the water touched our knees. It was kind of scary. At first the water was cold, but after a few minutes, we got used to the temperature. Standing on the edge of the Burrowsville beach was dangerous. We hoped none of the fish came out of the water to attack us. We couldn't help but to smile at each other. There were lots of people on the beach and in the water. Out into the bay, we could see them in their boats. We could see some of them pull fish out of the water, using these long strings of rope.

As we were standing up to our knees in the water, we met a girl named Sally, who liked to collect shells. She had collected some that are rare and very valuable. She earned money from them. She told us not to be afraid of the water. She must have noticed the fright on our faces as we stared out into Burnaby Bay. She loved to collect shells from the sea. She showed us some of them. She asked us if we wanted to buy some. We didn't have any vouchers, so we couldn't.

Petrina and I decided to come out of the shallow water, and we started walking toward the souvenir shops further along the beach. Pepper and Pickle wanted to come with us too, so we walked for about ten minutes along the seashore. It was such a nice day. We met Peter and Piper, who were already inside a souvenir shop. But we really couldn't buy anything there either, because we didn't have any vouchers. Then we heard Mr. Pumpkin shout from a distance. It was time to return home. We started walking back up the stairs where the bus was parked, in the parking lot. We noticed many pumpkins were loading back onto the buses.

"We have to get some souvenirs or a memento from this day, Pannette," said Pepper.

"What about the shells? Let's ask Mr. Pumpkin if we can get some seashells from that girl."

"Mr. Pumpkin, we still need a souvenir. Can we buy some seashells from a girl on the beach? She is way over there," I asked Mr. Pumpkin.

He said yes, but we had to hurry, because we were to leave soon. He gave vouchers to Piper and instructed her to escort us. But from our visual, I didn't even see her near the water, where she was standing before.

"Who are you talking about?" asked Pickle.

"There was a girl back there selling seashells. We want some, as souvenirs. It would be such a shame if we left Burrowsville without bringing home any souvenirs."

Peter and Pickle needed a souvenir also.

"I'll meet you back on the bus then," confirmed Petrina. "I want a window seat. Make sure you get me a real nice seashell, okay?"

So Peter, Piper, Pickle, Pepper, and I went back to see if she was still selling seashells by the seashore. And she was. We found her. She still had so many shells in her possession. She had periwinkle shells, cone shells, shark eye shells, branded tulips, jingles, and angel wings. She had so many. I selected a beautiful shell called knobby whelk. And I picked out a wentletrap shell for Petrina. While Piper was giving the girl the necessary vouchers, we noticed Pebbles still on the beach. Pebbles refused to leave. She was buried underneath the sand. She had spent this whole time lying and rolling around in the sand.

"This is where I belong. I don't want to go. The sand is so warm on my skin," she pleaded.

So I left our group to help Ms. Pumpkin convince Pebbles to leave the beach. Paris and Pompeo came to help as well. It looked like Ms. Pumpkin needed all the assistance she could get. Pebbles was practically throwing a tantrum. We had to almost carry her back onto the bus. She was crying loudly and showed considerable resistance. But we managed to get her back on the bus and into a seat. She was really depressed.

"I want to go back. I want to go play in the sand. That's where I belong," she cried.

Piper had filled up a bag of sand and gave it to Pebbles. She grasped onto it with dear life, opening the bag, and sticking her nose inside to smell the aroma.

Pashelle was upset as well. She sat on the bus with her arms folded. I wonder what happened. Petrina said she had an argument with Portia. I asked Pashelle about it, and she wouldn't tell me. Petrina didn't know what it was about either. It seemed like whenever Portia was around, it brought out the worst in Pashelle.

"Why aren't we moving?" someone asked.

"We're still waiting for one more pumpkin."

"Who?"

"Pandora. She lost her box."

"What?"

"Remember we had to empty our sacs and open up any bags when we went in the zoo? Well, Pandora didn't want to open up her box. And she wasn't allowed to bring it inside with her. So she left it at the reception area. And we think they lost it."

"Aw!" we exclaimed.

"Oh. Here she comes."

She seemed flustered. She was mad. She seemed livid. She stared right at me with her dark eyes as she passed by me on the bus aisle. She found a seat right behind me, next to Peter. She wasn't happy at all. But at least she had her box. They found it. I couldn't imagine how upset she would have been if they hadn't found it.

"People are so disorganized. It's unbelievable. You leave something at checkout. They say they will hold it for you. Then they lose it? Absolutely ridiculous. They almost lost by box. I almost had a heart attack. They better not have opened it and looked inside," she ranted.

Just relax, Pandora, I felt like saying. I mean, she's got her box. And besides, she doesn't even know what's in it. She was told by some ghost like creature to never open it. Why didn't she just leave it back at the patch? Why did she carry it around with her all the time? My goodness. All we could hear was Pandora ranting as the bus driver slowly pulled out of the parking lot of the Burrowsville Water Park and Zoo.

I sat next to Petrina. We were looking at each other, almost in amazement. Pebbles was still crying. She was sitting next to Pavneet across the aisle from us. Pavneet had to console her. She had her arms around her. Pashelle was in front of us. She kept saying, "Leave me alone" to Polo, who was sitting next to her. And Pandora was sitting behind us. She continued on her rant. She started to complain about other things, like what people were doing about the fallen werewolves. "Apparently, absolutely nothing. People have no sense of responsibility," she continued.

"And when there is another full moon, they're going to fall again. And is anyone going to do anything about it? The whole werewolf population is going extinct, and no one cares."

Peter had to take a break from her. He learned forward to ask Petrina about Halloween night. Was it a full moon that day? Petrina didn't know. Neither did I. "Was it a full moon on New Year's Eve?" he asked again. We didn't know. "On which day are we having our games?" We didn't know the answer to that question either.

As soon as we arrived back at Linden Road, Peter bolted from the bus and ran away. He said something like, "We need to talk to William. We can finally respond to his request." What request? What was he up to? I wasn't too concerned. After all, his behavior could be unpredictable.

It was a long day, and it was late. It was dinnertime. None of us were hungry though. We had all eaten quite a full lunch. My friends and I went to Pashelle's house to hang out, since we were so close. Her brothers and sisters were home. We talked and played card games. When it got really late, we all left and went home. When I got home, I told Patrick and Parson about my day. I showed them my sea shells and placed them on my bedside table. They didn't seem too interested though. Oh well. But at least it was a fun day.

CHAPTER 10
GAMES OF SUMMER

Weeks had passed. The school year was coming to a close. There were only a few more days of in-class training. Our daily walking and jogging exercises had turned into marathons and sprints. We would jog for twenty minutes nonstop on some days. And on other days, we would race for twenty-five meters, fifty meters, or even one hundred meters.

Ms. Pumpkin started to recap all of the things we had learned during the year. I had completely forgotten some of the things we had learned at the beginning of the school year, and it was difficult to relearn them. At least there was no more new material.

It was sunny every day. Our patch looked beautiful. The gardens were full of flowers. When you walked around the eye, the smell of the flowers was overwhelming. The gardeners did such a nice job. It would be fun to volunteer as a gardener.

We started to prepare for the annual fun and competitive events, which led to the conclusion of our school year. We called them our games of summer. They were a collection of individual and team races and other events. That meant a lot more physical activity. We had to sign up for the events we wanted to participate in. We had to pick a team name. Pashelle was adamant our team name should be called "the Warlocks." Petrina had suggested "the Witches," but Pashelle thought it would please Wanda Witch, knowing we had emulated her. None of us minded being called the Warlocks. Our team consisted of our class members.

On the day before the games, we set up the fields for the events. We put up orange markers where they needed to be. We put up signs at the appropriate places. The grounds needed to be cleaned. The golf course had to be resodded. Our class spent the whole school day preparing for the games. In actual fact, many other pumpkins had spent the whole week preparing—pumpkins of all ages. The elders helped to organize the activities.

But on the morning of the games, after we had put on our colored bibs and were assembled in front of the school, it was announced that the games had to be delayed. They would be moved to the following week. Ms. Pumpkin explained that paint was accidentally spilled on the ribbons. It was only discovered that morning. They needed to be cleaned. We couldn't have the games without the ribbons. The ribbons were essential, we were told. They held symbolic importance. These ribbons were hundreds and hundreds of years old, passed down from past generations. So as much as I was dreading the physical activity, it was still a disappointment because instead of spending the day outside, we spent the day inside—studying. It seemed that all the preparation we had done was a waste of time. I myself wasn't sure why we couldn't just have the games without the ribbons. I mean, I didn't think I was going to win a ribbon anyways. At least we did not have to take apart all the work we had done the previous day. The elders decided to leave the markers and the signs as they were. Pumpkins probably had to reline the fields though.

Some elders were very disappointed. Ms. Patricia Pumpkin seemed particularly upset. I mean, delaying the games just because the ribbons needed cleaning seemed rash. I could see her point. Some of the other elected elders seemed pleased though. Ms. Poppy Pumpkin, Ms. Pinky Pumpkin, and Mr. Percival Pumpkin said it was for the best. Peter made it known to everyone that delaying the games was the best course of action. I'm sure he didn't feel like running and doing all that exercise either.

The elders didn't want any pumpkin messing with the markers and signs and wanted to keep all the work we had done intact. We were told to stay clear from this area. Furthermore, we were told that no one should be outside that evening. That request seemed rather strange. I mean, why couldn't we be outside on such a beautiful summer day? The elders never really explained that to us. We would spend the rest of the school day inside, studying.

"Make sure you all stay indoors," we were reminded as we left school on that day.

My friends and I decided to go back to my place. And that evening, would you believe there were more lightning strikes? And again, there were very few clouds in the sky. And there was no thunder afterward.

"This is crazy,"

"I know, right?"

"Is this lightning ever going to stop?"

"Where is it coming from?"

"How come there is no rain?"

The strikes lasted for a few minutes. But this time, they were different. They were like half lightning. They came halfway down the sky, they stopped, and then they seem to have gone right back upward again. They went in reverse. We could see the lightning go back upward. And after a few minutes, there was a big explosion in the sky. Wow! My goodness. It was like a loud bomb. Everyone must have seen it. Smoke had littered the sky, as if there had been a giant fire.

"Did you see that?"

"That was the weirdest thing I have ever seen."

It was only a few more minutes after the giant explosion when Mr. Pumpkin knocked on the door and said that everyone should go home.

After the weekend, on the next school day, all the pumpkins in the patch were summoned to the arena for a meeting. And it was sad news. Ms. Pumpkin announced that when the lightning struck earlier, during spring break, it had damaged the pumpkin seeds. There would only be one new pumpkin born this year. That was sad. It was a tragedy. A whole generation of pumpkins lost, even before given a chance at life. That was probably why some elders were so sad during that time. It had been discovered during spring break.

And there was a second announcement. It was confirmed that no one had stolen the exams after all. The lightning strike at the storage site killed the exams. It was explained to us that the strike had taken out all of the wording from the papers. The exams had died. All of the life was sucked out of the papers. The words had been erased. This was the only plausible explanation.

She also had good news to report as well, relating to all of this, but nothing could be confirmed at that point in time. It was very mysterious. She was purposely being careful to not provide any more details than were necessary.

The third announcement was that the games of summer were back on for the upcoming Friday.

School was cancelled for the day. Again. We were all encouraged to go home and study.

"On this Friday ... isn't it Friday the thirteenth?" remarked Pavneet as we left the school building. "That's kind of scary. With all of the crazy lightning, why in the world would we have the games of summer on Friday the thirteenth?"

She was right. Strange things always seemed to happen to pumpkins on a Friday that falls on the thirteenth day of the month. I wondered if strange things happened to other species too. Probably not. I was sure it was just a pumpkin superstition.

"Isn't it too bad about the seeds? So the lightning hit the seeds, and that's why they went bad?" asked Pavneet to confirm.

"And that's why the exams had turned into blank sheets of paper," added Peter.

But the games were back on. Every pumpkin was excited about that. I signed up to participate in four individual events. I tried to pick the easiest events to enter.

There were individual awards, and there were team awards. The ribbons had been cleaned. They were as good as new. It was class 1 versus class 2 versus class 3. The spirit of competition was encouraged. In good fun, of course. Class 2 decided on "the Stems" as their team name, while class 3 chose "Orange Glow."

When we met at the school grounds on Friday the thirteenth, my friends and I immediately viewed the race event order to see when we would all participate.

The first event was the marathon. From the Warlocks, Pippi and Pippa were the two who raced. They would run three times around the soccer field and golf course. We were told it would take them almost half an hour. That is a long journey. I could never do something like that. As they started, Pudge declared, "The games of summer are on." He loved saying that.

I walked with Plato and Picasso to one side of the grounds to prepare for my first event. It was bobbing for apples. Other pumpkins went to the table tennis tables, while other pumpkins started jumping on the trampoline.

I did fairly well at bobbing. Elders tied my hands behind my back and placed a blindfold over my eyes, so I couldn't see what I was doing. Then I had to dunk my face into a barrel of water, trying to bite on and secure as many apples out of the barrel as possible in seven minutes. It was very tricky. I was the first to participate. I pulled out eleven apples. It was very difficult to bite into them because when I felt one and tried to bite into the apple, it floated away. I got the third most apples. That meant I was awarded a third-place ribbon! I was so happy. I was very proud of myself. Plato retrieved five apples, while Picasso was able to secure four. As a team, we finished last. Or as we are supposed to say, we finished third. We got zero points as a team. The first place team received five points for all events. The second place team would receive two points. Petrina came up to me and told me she came in fourth in the trampoline. I showed her my third-place ribbon. She gave me one of her sarcastic smiles.

By the time Pavneet came racing into pumpkin headquarters after completing her marathon, four events were complete. Due to Pavneet's performance, Orange Glow won the marathon. They also won the table tennis event. The Stems won the bobbing and trampoline events. And after the first four events of the games of summer, the standings were:

Orange Glow: 12
The Stems: 10
The Warlocks: 6

Our team had finished second in three of the events. Then the five-year-olds took a break. We watched some of the other pumpkins participate in their events. Petrina, Pavneet, Pashelle, and I thought the three-legged race was the most adventurous and fun. Pumpkins raced in pairs, with rope tied to hold their legs together. They had to run in unison. We laughed when we saw Patrick and Parson stumble over each other just as they reached the finish line.

I also watched Polo use a wooden club to pound onto a small rubber ball, which forced another rubber ball to shoot upward. The rubber ball was measured for height. The harder Polo hit the first rubber ball, the second would rise accordingly. He had swung the club and hit the ball with quite a bit of power. From a distance, I couldn't quite see exactly how high the second rubber ball reached, but I'm sure he won that event. It was part of the strong pumpkin competition. They also threw spears and threw tiny but heavy steel balls.

Then I turned my attention to our turn at the three-legged race. Pippa and Pippi finished third. Peter and Petrina finished last. Those two ran awkwardly. Petrina seemed a bit perturbed with Peter. The Warlocks finished third in the three-legged race, but we won the strong man competition. The standings after the first six events were:

Orange Glow: 16
The Stems: 15
The Warlocks: 11

Then we took another break. The next events were the running races, but the ten-year-old pumpkins were still using that part of the field. So we had to wait. We ate food. We drank. We had a great time. Petrina had noticed my purple bow was no longer on my stem.

"Oh no. I wonder if it fell off when I was bobbing for apples," I said.

"Go check with Ms. Pumpkin. Check in the barrel."

I loved wearing my purple bow. I always had one tied to my stem. I went to go ask Ms. Pumpkin. She said they emptied and rinsed out the barrels quite frequently, to ensure the water was always clean and fresh. My purple bow was probably in the garbage. So I had to make a decision. Should I quickly go home and get another one of my purple bows? Or should I just forget about it. I had to make a decision quickly, because the next events would start sooner rather than later. I really felt awkward without my purple bow. I felt out of sorts—misplaced, almost. So I decided to race home.

"I'll be back in a minute!" I yelled out to Petrina and Pashelle. I raced over the Water Gate Bridge. I raced through the gardens of the eye. Then south down column CD03, then I turned on TY07. I noticed Mr. Pumpkin sitting on his doorstep, but I obviously had no time to chat. I grabbed another purple bow from my drawer. I was in and out of my house in a heartbeat. As I closed my front door, I heard Mr. Pumpkin say hello. "Oh hello," I replied. Or did he say "help"?

"Are you okay?" I asked him. He had one hand on his chest. He seemed to be grasping for air. It looked like he needed help.

"Are you okay?" I asked him again.

"I don't know. I don't think so."

I noticed seeds dripping out of his mouth. That didn't look good. That looked ugly.

"Wait right here. I'm going to get help for you," I said. His skin felt so cold.

I raced back to the eye as quickly as I could. I had to rest on a bench in the green garden for a minute. It was only sheer adrenaline that enabled me to cross the Water Gate Bridge. I got the attention of the nearest elder I could find. I found myself almost out of breath. That trip must have taken over thirty minutes. I wondered if I had missed any of my events.

"Ms. Pumpkin ... Ms. Pumpkin. I think that ..."

"Pannette! Pannette! Over here. Come on. The relay is starting. We need you," screamed Pashelle.

Our next race was about to start. And it was the relay. I didn't want to let my team down, so I raced to where my teammates were. I was in the hundred-meter relay. There were four of us in the relay. I was really nervous about this race. So much pressure to live up to other pumpkins' expectations of you.

"I'll go first," announced Pashelle. She took hold of a racing baton that she would pass onward to the next racer. Good. It would give me time to rest for a minute. Plus I still needed to tie on my purple bow.

"I want to go last. I want to cross the finish line when we are winning," said Polo.

"I can go third," said Pebbles.

Okay. Great. Then I was second.

We each took our appropriate place on the race track. We started cheering Pashelle on, when the race started. Run Pashelle. Run. Faster. As she came running toward me, when she turned the corner on the race track oval, she gave me the baton. I clutched it with dear life and started running as fast as I could. We were in first place. But by the time I gave the baton to Pebbles, we were in last place. But not by very much. By the time Polo got the baton, we were quite far behind. Pebbles didn't run much faster than I did. But Polo sprinted like a cheetah, like we were told at the zoo, and our team ended up in second place.

We continued on with the running portion of the games. Next was the hundred-meter dash. Pavneet came in first. Because of her performance, Orange Glow won first place. Pavneet also won the fifty-meter dash. I think she would have won the thirty-meter dash also, but she didn't participate in that event. Instead Polo won. I participated in the thirty-meter dash, and I finished in the middle of the pack. I had become so tired by that time. I had very little energy. That trip back to my house didn't help. But we won first place, as a team. And the standings after ten events were:

Orange Glow: 31
The Stems: 21
The Warlocks: 18

We had fallen quite far behind. It was a bit disappointing. But we were having so much fun that we really didn't care about the standings. I didn't anyway. It wasn't about the winning. Besides, the only reason why Orange Glow was so far ahead was because of Pavneet. She had entered into four events and had finished first all four times.

The next event was the hurdles. It was like a running race, but pumpkins had to jump over and dodge various obstacles that were in the way. And good for Petrina. She finished in second place. She received a second place ribbon. I was so happy for her. Her face was beaming. She couldn't believe it. Many of the pumpkins in the race had all kinds of difficulty. It was quite funny. There were only a few lanes in which they ran, unlike the other races. And they all tripped over each other and tumbled. Pavneet ended up winning quite easily. She had just won her fifth first-place ribbon. Pippa finished third, and it drew us a little closer. The standings were now:

Orange Glow: 31
The Stems: 23
The Warlocks: 23

We then took a break for lunch. We needed a break after all the excitement. I needed to calm down. It seemed that I had a smile on my face the whole day. While we ate, we watched all the other pumpkins participate in their events.

After lunch, we headed to the rolling hills. We five-year-olds all rolled at the same time. Thirty-two pumpkins were aligned at the top of the hill, and we all rolled down together. Pebbles and Polo finished first and second, respectively. I finished a disappointing thirty-first. I only finished ahead of Peter. He wiped out again and finished last. He ended up rolling outside the orange markers, which were considered out of bounds. Penny had injured her ankle during the hurdle event, so she did not participate. And our team drew even closer to first. The team standings were now:

Orange Glow: 33
The Warlocks: 28
The Stems: 23

Then we went to the golf course to perform various golf drills. We didn't play the full eighteen-hole course though. Instead, we assembled on the seventeenth hole. I participated in the golf event. I had to hit a golf ball out of a sand trap, to try to get it as close to the hole as possible, if not in. I didn't do very well for that shot. I only got the ball out of the sand trap on my fourth try. But I made a great putt. And it was almost a fluke, as I had my eyes closed when I putted. I gave the ball a good whack. And it went in the hole! My goodness! I sank a thirteen footer! Because of that, I got my second ribbon. I finished in second place. And just like that, we were tied for first place in the team standings.

Each time our team did well, Pom Pom led a cheer. She started twirling around a baton like stick, made of wood, in her dance act. And Polka, who was one year younger, would join her in the dancing. Polka convinced many of the four-year-olds to support and cheer for the Warlocks, so we ended up having a large contingent of the four-year-olds rooting for our team, including Purvis, Perkins, Prescott, Peaches, Pillow, Pony, Pimi, and Pazzy P.

We then played soccer. We played each of the other teams. Each game was twenty minutes. We played the Stems first, and we won. Then we took a break and watched a wild 3–3 game between Orange

Glow and the Stems. In our second game, we were losing 1–0, when
Peter scored the equalizer right at the end of the game. We tied the
game, just in the nick of time. We finished with one win and one tie,
and that was good enough to earn us the five points. And just like
that, we were ahead in the team standings, heading into the final
event of the day. It was the tug of war.

The top two teams qualified for the tug of war. Whoever won
this event would win the overall team competition. We had to wait
for a few minutes, while the gardeners prepared the grounds and
sand. The gardeners had prepared this area for weeks. They took
out the grass. It was called artificial grass—not real grass. And they
poured in sand. So they were evening out the sand because the six-
year-olds had just finished.

I chatted with Palmer while we waited.

"So how are things in Ms. Pumpkin's class?" he asked.

"Good. It was too bad that you had to move. I know you liked
talking to Petrina."

"It was for the best. I'm actually glad. I think things weren't going
so well with her and me, so I asked Ms. Pumpkin if I could move."

"Yeah. So the note really worked then … Wait. What? You asked
to be moved?"

"Yes. I thought that Petrina and I would be better friends if I
wasn't in her face all the time. That's what she told me—that I was
'in her face all the time.'"

"Good."

"What note?" he asked. Then after a pause, he said, "Ms. Pumpkin
mentioned a note too, I recall. But I didn't pay much attention to
what she said. I mean, you don't mean that note I wrote to Petrina.
I threw that away. Did Ms. Pumpkin get her hands on that note?"

I cannot believe I just mentioned the note. A slip of the tongue.
Terrible slip.

"No. No one has seen that note, Palmer. Never mind. Everything has worked out really well, then. That is really good news."

I really didn't want to talk to him about his move.

Then it was time to start the tug of war. Thank goodness. "Come on, Palmer. You're on the other side."

All twenty-two of us started pulling, tugging, and almost willing the rope to come our way. Eleven of us were pulling it one way, while eleven other pumpkins were pulling it the other way. It was physically and mentally tiring. I was exhausted even before the tug of war started. We pulled on that rope as hard as we could. After a few minutes of battle, Peter lost his footing and slipped. He ended falling to one side and rolled up on Pippi's leg. She then fell, and pretty soon, we all lost control of the rope. We ended up stumbling over each other. In the end Pippa and Pashelle were the only two holding our end of the rope. They got dragged over the finish line in no time. We all started laughing. Orange Glow won the tug of war and the team competition.

In a surprise move, some of the Orange Glow team members, including Panic and Plunder, grabbed one of the barrels of water and poured it over Ms. Pumpkin's head. She was in shock. She became drenched. The water seemed cold. It was all in good fun.

Pavneet won the award for best athlete. She was awarded the coveted golden medal. That was a no brainer. She was the only athlete to win six first-place orange ribbons. Pele was awarded the silver medal, and Parker was awarded the bronze medal.

We had a great party afterward too, for all the pumpkins. We all had a blast, dancing and partying, and playing games in and around the school grounds. And it was such a nice sunny day outside, too. I had so much fun that day that it may have been one of the happiest days of my life. It was a day that I will never forget.

CHAPTER 11
HOMEWORK

The next morning, I was forced to wake early. I was still tired from all the exercising the previous day. My arms and legs were sore. My body was all swollen. I tensed up. I saw Patrick straighten up from his bed. We heard an incredible collection of loud shrieks outside. They were from the ghouls. I gasped, barely able to breathe. It seemed like the ghouls were right above our house. Then they stopped, all at once. It was almost like a morning wake-up call. We were all forced to wake. I made eye contact with my two brothers. Pillow was quite startled as she had grabbed onto my right arm. Patrick was the first to rise from bed, and he opened our front door. Parson and I soon joined him. It was barely light outside. The sun was just beginning to rise. We found numerous pieces of paper littered all over the place. My goodness. What in the world was going on? I picked up one of the pieces of paper. Something was written on it, but none of us knew what it meant, though, as the writing was weird. It wasn't even in English but some strange language. It was very odd. We looked up, and we could see hundreds and hundreds of bats, werewolves, ghosts, and other ghouls in the sky. It was kind of scary. Once they saw pumpkins come out of their houses, they all left from our view at the same time. We always saw ghouls flying overhead. However, on this occasion, there were so many of them hovering over us all at once.

"What does the note mean?" asked Peaches, who was standing near the doorway.

Since we noticed all our neighbors going back inside their houses, we didn't pay it any extra attention. We went back inside and tried to go back to sleep, since it couldn't have been more than six o'clock in the morning. We didn't want to give the notes any attention. But it was no use.

"Let's go to the eye," I suggested.

Good idea. I was always coming up with good ideas. I mean, it seemed the most logical thing to do. Why would we wait here to find out what that ghoul gathering was all about? As we walked north on column TY07, we were joined by many pumpkins that morning. And when we passed through the west gate, we saw hundreds of pumpkins all over the eye gardens. Everyone was asking about the notes. The patch was littered with them.

"I always thought that ghouls couldn't fly over the trees and look down into our patch," said Petrina, who came up from behind me.

"Me neither," I confirmed.

"The elders only say that to make us feel safer," said Prospero.

"The trees aren't that tall," added Pimlico.

"Do you know what's going on with the notes?" I asked.

"The language is so strange," added Petrina.

"I just saw Mr. Pumpkin go into the office. They'll figure it out. Someone will be able to read the language," replied Pimlico. "I'm sure they'll be some kind of an announcement."

And sure enough, Ms. Pumpkin came walking out of the office. When she reached the outer edge of the rose garden, she made a statement.

"We can confirm that the notes are written in werewolf. And they read, 'Thank you.' Now, we don't know exactly the reason why they sent these notes to us, but we have a very good idea. And we will gather as much information, and provide it to you, as it becomes available. In the meantime, please feel free to go home, and go back to sleep. It is early."

It was Saturday. No school on Saturdays. Actually, after the games, there would be no more formal sessions at school. It was the start of preparation for the final exams and practical tests. The final exam was to be written in three weeks. Then the school year would be over. Finally.

My friends and I decided to stay there. Polo, Plato, and Pashelle found us. And we saw Pavneet as soon as we entered the dining hall. Ms. Pumpkin started to prepare eggs and toast for anyone who wanted to stay and eat an early breakfast.

We had a conversation about the notes. We speculated about what the note could mean. Then we talked about the games. When there was a lull in the conversation, Plato suggested we all go to the library. We would all go home, collect our books, and meet back in the school library to study. After we had finished our breakfast, we agreed to the plan. I met my friends at the library, and we started to read over the material from the school year. It wasn't very long before I felt tired and drowsy. I had been awake for quite some time. Plus, I must have been coming down with a cold or something because I was unusually tired. All the reading made my head hurt. All my friends were reading. My mind began to wander.

I told my friends I was going home. I said I would meet up with everyone here, first thing the following morning, though, for a full session of studying.

But instead of going home, I decided to go to the lounge. I thought I would watch television. I mean, if everyone was studying then the television must be free. I watched for a couple of hours. Then I got bored and thought I would go home. But before I went home, I went to Pannette's Plateau. Actually this area of the patch did not have a name, so I called it Pannette's Plateau. It is a hill on the northeast corner of the eye. It's kind of a dangerous place to sit. We have to climb up a steep hill, to arrive at a jagged cliff. I come here sometimes when I want to be alone. I looked westward to see if I could spot the water park and zoo, but it was too far away to get a clear visual. I could see Romo Island off in the distance. The city looked nice. It was a bit of a bird's-eye view of the cars and the people in the streets. The city buildings seemed closer. You could see the reflection of the sun hitting the buildings, creating images onto Burnaby Bay. The city looked nice because the garbage and smell was too far away, no doubt. I gazed at the sky to see if I could see the sun moving down. I must have sat on those cliffs for hours, daydreaming, because the next thing I knew, it was dark. The sun had gone down. I decided to go back to the lounge, to see if my friends were there. I hadn't spoken to them since the morning.

They sure had a lot more information about the notes. It was crowded in the lounge.

"Pannette!" Petrina yelled. "Oh my God, where have you been all this time? I have to tell you what happened."

"Okay."

"Peter told us everything," she started.

"What did he say?"

"Peter and some of the elected elders were trying to figure out why all the werewolves started dying on full moons. There was a full moon on Halloween night, and they died. Same thing on New Year's Eve, and they died."

"Okay. Right."

"He said a werewolf told him that he got hit by the silver

lightning. The werewolf told him this when we went to the city. Do you remember? When that dog chased us. He was actually running to the fallen werewolf."

"No. I mean I was stuck in a sewer …"

"Peter got the doctors to test the seeds. And those seeds had been lost. Forever. All of the life was taken from them. No one stole the exam papers, Pannette. Do you remember? When it hit the school, it took all the life out of the paper. It erased all of the words. No one thinks anyone stole the exams now. It was all because of the lightning."

Okay. I listened in amazement to the story. Sometimes Pashelle was talking, and other times it was Petrina. They were practically interrupting each other.

"Peter thought that Wanda was the one who was creating the lightning. He was the first to point all of this out to the elders. Wanda got the power somehow. And Peter thought she was going to use the power to hit us on the games of summer. So Peter, Ms. Poppy, Ms. Pinky, and Mr. Percival wanted the games moved. They argued with all the elected elders. Peter said they accidentally, on purpose, spilled paint on the ribbons, so the elected elders had to move the games. The elected elders were left with no choice but to move the games. Pumpkins and the ghouls tricked Wanda."

"What do you mean?"

"They made Wanda think that we were having our games. But they got cancelled. And we had to cancel them, because they fell on a full moon. So on that day, William Werewolf, Victor Vampire, and Gillam Ghost devised a trap for Wanda. Ghoul scientists created a magic potion to shatter the silver bolt. Victor told Wanda that he wanted to see her power and instructed her to use it on the day we would have our games. He told her to wipe us all out with the strike. They set a trap for Wanda. The ghouls waited for Wanda to make the strike. They figured out that Wanda only had the capability to strike when there was a full moon. We were all inside. And when Wanda used her new power to strike the lightning, the scientists somehow caught the lightning and threw it back into the sky. They destroyed it. That is why there was that giant explosion. Do you remember? They reversed the power. They knew the lightning was coming. They knew exactly when. Now everyone thinks Wanda has lost her new power."

"My goodness." Petrina was talking so fast. She was so hyper.

"I know, right?"

"How did she get the power in the first place?" I asked.

"Some of the werewolves think she must have been the mysterious ghoul at Walden's funeral. They suspected, but they weren't sure. The ghoul was spotted at the funeral, near the apse, when William took command. Something may have happened there. That must have been Wanda."

"For sure it was. Isn't that strange that the vampires helped the werewolves? I mean those species are always fighting. We have been told they have been fighting for centuries," I said.

"The vampires and the other ghouls thought it was better to work with the werewolves, rather than allow Wanda to have this power."

"I thought Panic stole the exams. Panic was near the building when it happened, we were told. And why was Peter talking and screaming at Panic, later? Wasn't that about the exams?"

"No he wasn't. Peter was only upset at him because Panic was saying that his class was going to thrash us in the games. And Peter was getting mad at him, because Panic didn't show the right spirit. I mean the games are not about winning but trying your best and having fun."

"Wanda killed our pumpkin seeds. That makes me so mad," said Pavneet, who just joined us.

"Where did you go? You were right with me when we left the library."

"I had to go ask Portia something."

"Are you friends with her now?" asked Pashelle with a rude stare.

Pavneet ignored her. She continued on with the story.

"Peter argued with the elected elders, asking them to retest the seeds. But many elders didn't want to, because then they would have to dig them out of the ground. That's dangerous for the new seeds. But they did. They dug out a few of them, tested them, and they were almost dead. The doctors couldn't save them. That's why everyone was so sad, after spring break. The elders knew the pumpkin seeds had been lost."

"And the ghouls helped us."

"They had to. They had to stop Wanda. We all did."

"So that's why there were the notes. The ghouls sent down notes to thank us. They said that we were brave to put aside our differences and collaborate. They realized that collaboration to fight Wanda was the best thing."

"I wonder what's going to happen now."

"This is what I was just talking to Parker and Portia about. Victor wants the president to call Wanda to the tribunal. Victor wants Wanda to stand trial."

"Good."

"But we doubt that will happen. All the people want is to maintain the peace, so they might not force her. Besides, the warlocks are defending the witches. They are saying this is an internal issue."

"Wanda killed werewolves, and they are saying it is an internal issue? When did you find this out?"

"Just now. I wanted to ask Portia about something for school, but she was talking to some of the elected elders. And they just got word from Victor Vampire that he cannot get the president to assess charges."

"So after all of that, Wanda is still free?"

"It looks like it."

"At least we stopped her."

After a brief pause in the conversation, some pumpkins suggested we go home and get a good night's sleep and to meet back at the library first thing in the morning, so we could continue to study. It's called homework. I hate that word. We were to meet in the library each and every morning, until we wrote the final exam. All of my friends were so interested in the study material.

That was a lot of information to take in all at once. Wanda was so cruel. She murdered werewolves. She killed our baby pumpkin seeds. The whole situation was very troubling and sad. But we all had to let the issue go and move on with our lives and just be thankful that Wanda had finally lost her new power.

The next morning, when I arrived at the school grounds, Pavneet wanted me to come running with her and some other pumpkins. "You haven't come to run in such a long time," she noticed. But I was so tired, so I couldn't really. I didn't have the energy. Peter, Petrina, and Peanut wanted me to come with them to practice on the computer later, so I did. But there were so many pumpkins in the computer room that I really didn't get a chance to use any of them. I could never get my hands on one of the few cell phones we had.

I started spending afternoons with Plato, Polo, and Pashelle in a study group, concentrating on the items we learnt during species class. One afternoon I was reading, and then I fell asleep. I wished the final exam was over.

That evening I had spoken with Peaches. It was late at night. We were in my bed. Pillow, Patrick, and Parson had fallen asleep.

"I haven't seen Mr. Pumpkin in a while. I normally see him on the doorstep, but he is never there anymore. Does he just stay inside now?" I whispered. Probably so, because it was starting to get hot outside. He probably wanted to stay inside, to stay cool.

"Oh. Not really Pannette." She hesitated.

"Why? How come?"

She sniffled her nose. It sounded like she started to cry. I didn't mean for her to cry. I just wondered where he was.

"Are you okay, Peaches?"

"He died, Pannette."

Aw.

"Oh. That's so sad. I'm sorry. When did this happen?"

"On the games of summer. Pillow found him that evening. He was just sitting, kind of crumpled over to one side. So Pillow went to go get Dr. Pumpkin. And he said he just died. I miss him. Pillow does too. We all do."

Why didn't she tell me this before? I mean I saw him during the games of summer. Didn't I? I can't remember. I did. I'm sure I did. I was about to utter this comment to Peaches, but I didn't. Instead I listened to her. She started explaining how he had spent the final few days of his life.

My mind started to wonder. I had completely forgotten. I did meet him, when I went back to retrieve a purple bow. He needed help. Did I get him help? I did. I told Ms. Pumpkin. Didn't I? I'm sure I did. And he died that night?

Didn't I do anything to help him? I suddenly realized I didn't. My mind went blank. All I could picture was his face on that day and how he looked so tired and cold.

Peaches eventually stopped talking and crying. She fell asleep.

I was in shock almost. I didn't know what to do or think. I mean, there was nothing I could do now. I should have done something then. Tears started to roll down from my eyes. I had to wipe them away with the palm of my hand.

He said he was so cold. I didn't even give him a blanket.

CHAPTER 12

STUDY

I was tired of lying on my bed, so I got up and sat outside my door for a few hours. It was really early in the morning. It was still dark, but I could see the sun start to rise. The weather was so nice—so warm and cool at the same time. I sat just and wondered about Mr. Pumpkin. I couldn't stop thinking about him. Even after I went back inside and laid on my bed, I was never able to fall asleep. I'm not even sure if I slept at all that evening.

Parson was to first to wake up and then Patrick soon after.

For some reason, I didn't want to be alone that day. I didn't want to walk to the school library by myself, so I got up too. I quickly prepared myself for the school day.

"I'll walk with you to school today," I said to my two brothers.

I listened to their conversation on the way to school. It was nice to hear their voices. Once we entered the eye, they ran away. They went to meet up with their friends.

I continued on toward the library. I wanted to tell someone about Mr. Pumpkin. I thought I would tell Petrina, but I couldn't find her inside. So I started to walk back toward the west gate and wait for her to come through. It took a while, but she came through the gate. She was walking with Peter. As soon as I got near them though, Petrina bolted off. She said she had to go. I wanted to say, "Wait, I have to tell you something." I hesitated and missed my chance.

"I wanted to tell her something," I whispered to myself.

"What did you want to say?" Peter asked.

"Oh nothing."

"Okay."

I stood there for a minute. I thought Peter would walk away, but he stayed. He lingered. It felt awkward. I really didn't want to walk with him. Didn't he have anywhere to go? I started walking back toward the library. Peter didn't leave my side though. I felt like saying something to someone.

"Mr. Pumpkin was sick, and I didn't help him. He died. It was my fault," I finally blurted out.

He looked at me and almost knew who I was referring to. "Do you mean Mr. Pumpkin who lives with Pillow?" he asked.

I nodded.

"I was with Dr. Pumpkin that night. He was showing me the types of tests they conducted on the pumpkin seeds. And then Pillow came running up, and told us about his condition, so we went to go see Mr. Pumpkin. We brought him back to the hospital. He was old Pannette. His skin had become so soft. He had lost all of his color. There was nothing you could have done."

"I could have. I saw him that day. I knew he was sick. I could have given him a blanket. I'm not even sure if I told anyone," I confessed. "I didn't even try to help. And now I can't do anything about it. It's too late."

"It's never too late to help someone, Pannette," he reasoned. "From this day forward, you can try to help other pumpkins so they can live longer and healthier lives. I think a lot of pumpkins want you to help."

"But how can I help other pumpkins get better? They won't even let me help in the hospital. And you never help me," I said.

"I will help you, Pannette. But first, you have to try. Tell me you want to try."

"What?"

"Tell me you want to try."

"Okay. I will try."

I had started to become emotional. I mean, I did want to try. There was nothing else that was more important in my life.

He stared at me for a second and then took my school bag. He told me to wait there. By this time we had crossed the water gate and were approaching the school library. A few minutes passed. Then Pavneet came out of the school building and started walking toward me.

"Hi!" she said. "Are you ready?"

"Ready for what?" I asked. I had to take a heavy sigh, as I had gotten a little emotional. I didn't want to start crying in front of Pavneet. I had to try to recompose myself. Where did Peter go? And what did Pavneet want to do?

"Then let's go. Follow me."

She started to run. She said it was a light jog. It didn't seem like a light jog, as I had to almost race just to keep up with her. I wondered where we were going. I couldn't keep up with her. I had to stop. She also then stopped a few meters ahead of me. "Come on. We'll go slower today," she said.

What did she mean today? I was supposed to be meeting with Peter. Or was I? He took my school bag. All that running was making me sick. We had to rest quite a few times. Why were we jogging in the first place? Where were we going? I kept asking her, and she kept saying that we were almost there. After a while, I became tired of asking her. I was too tired to speak. She ended up doing most of the talking. We didn't stop until we had made one full lap around the school. We ended up right back where we had started.

Then she told me that she had to leave. As she walked away, she gave me instructions to be here the following morning, and we would run again. I didn't even have time or the energy to say no before she left my sight. I collapsed on the soft warm grass, to regain my strength. That run was ugly. I thought she wanted to run with me every day. I was not sure. I was not sure if I could run like this every day. I couldn't do that.

I had to find my school bag. But I was too tired. I needed to rest.

Then Plato came and sat down next to me on the grass. He had his math book with him. He told me he needed my help with something. He opened the book to page 1 and began to explain something to me. I listened to him. I was gaining my strength back. My legs didn't feel so achy anymore. It was nice sitting outside in the sun. One hour must have passed by. He was showing me formulas and equations and calculations. Then all of a sudden, he stopped at page 5. Just like that. He thanked me for listening to him. And then he left.

Just as he left, Pebbles and Popeye came closer to my view. They said they wanted to talk to me about something. Well I certainly was popular that day, wasn't I? I didn't even notice where Plato had gone. I should have asked him to find my school bag.

Pebbles, Popeye, and I walked toward the rolling hill. Popeye stopped at the bottom of the hill, while Pebbles led me up to the top. Well what did they want to talk to me about? Why was Pebbles taking me up to the top of the hill?

"Hey, Pebbles. What are we doing here?"

When we got to the top, she got on her knees and looked down toward the bottom of the hill.

"When you roll down the hill, start like this. On your knees.

Don't sit down on your bottom, because from this position, it's easier to tuck your legs inside your body than it would be if you started while sitting down. Okay? Come on. Let's go."

I think she wants to roll. Sure, I thought. *I have nothing else to do.* So I got on my knees.

"Now bend your neck only slightly. It's just as important to keep your head up, to ensure you are going straight. Then after the first roll, tuck your arms and legs inside. The quicker you can do this, the faster you will roll. So are we ready to go?"

This must have been at least my eighth trip down the hill.

"I think this is my tenth trip down the hill," I said.

"Oh really! Wow!"

"How many times have you rolled?"

"Oh, I don't know. I would guess over two hundred times." And with that comment, down the hill she went. My goodness. There was no hesitation at all. She took off like a rocket.

I braced myself, and down I went too. I made sure I followed her instructions. I seemed to roll faster. And I made sure to keep my head up, to go straight.

When I got to the bottom of the hill, I was still just as dazed and out of balance as all the other times. Popeye was there to greet me. I realized then that there were other pumpkins on the hill. Funny I never noticed them when we walked up. As Popeye was giving me some more tips on form and structure, I saw Perses come down the hill. And when he got up, he raised his arms up into the air, as if he had won some kind of prize. He didn't need to rest to regain his balance. He didn't feel dizzy. He didn't feel dizzy at all. He actually had fun. He seemed so happy.

Popeye then asked if I was listening to him.

"Did you hear what I said, Pannette?"

"Yes, Popeye."

"This was your fastest time."

This may have been my fastest time, but I still felt just as dizzy.

Pebbles then said she was really hungry and wanted to go eat. Sure. I agreed, even though it seemed a bit too early. At the school cafeteria, when we formed into the serving line, I noticed there was no one seated at the tables. I think we came a bit too early. There were quite a few pumpkins in line though. The food trays hadn't been lifted yet. So we waited.

Then Peter walked toward us, from the front of the line. He gave me my school bag. My goodness. I thought I had lost it. Or he lost it.

"We're in line, up this way," he said.

So Pebbles and I passed the many pumpkins in the line, and we stood with Peter, Porter, Penny, and Peanut.

We ate a nice meal. Then Pebbles had to go.

"Pannette, I want to show you something on the computer," said Porter. "It's this really cool picture that Picasso wanted me to draw."

So after we ate, we all went to the computer room. While most of the pumpkins were still eating, or in line getting food, we left the cafeteria and went to the computer room. And for a change, there was hardly anyone there. I could never seem to get my hands on any of the computers, because they were always in use. Picasso and Pashelle were the only ones in the room. They had the computer turned on. It looked like they were playing a card game. I think that's what people refer to as "online gambling."

Porter had turned on another computer and was trying to get my attention.

"Hey Pannette. Look at this picture Picasso drew for me. Now I am going to draw this same picture, but on this computer. And then we are going to print it out and hang both of these in my house."

He started showing me these screens and all these different websites. Then we watched Porter and Picasso try to replicate the same picture onto the computer, to match what was drawn on the sheet of paper. But Porter wasn't doing a very good job, so Picasso took over. Porter was showing Picasso how to use the buttons, top tabs, and coloring keys. And Picasso was creating a much better picture. Peanut and Penny were offering suggestions on how the new picture should look. I just watched.

"You are magical with the computer, Porter," said Penny.

"You should ask him, Pannette. See all the amazing things that Porter can do on a computer," added Peter.

Just then, Ms. Pumpkin came into the room.

"Peter. There you are. Come with me. Victor Vampire wants to speak with you. And he only wants to speak with you. Did you talk to the president when you were in the city? Victor says he saw you through a window. And you shook hands with the president."

"I don't think so. He wants to talk to me? Really?"

Wow. Peter shook hands with the president? When was this? And now Victor Vampire wanted to talk to him?"

Just as Peter and Ms. Pumpkin left the room, Pecan, Pandria, and Patience came into the room.

"Hey, Pannette. Let's go to the school cafeteria. Let's eat dessert. Pecan is going to bake her new dessert. The one she has been thinking about for weeks. Ms. Pumpkin finally has all of the correct ingredients."

Sure, I thought. I said bye to everyone in the computer room, and the four of us went into the school kitchen. Ms. Pumpkin handed Pecan some flour, and we saw Pecan mold the dough with her hands. Then she mixed in all her ingredients, including these special nuts that she craved so much. She made three different types of desserts, each one of them baked with different ingredients.

After she put the desserts in the oven, we helped Ms. Pumpkin clean the kitchen. It can get very dirty and messy in the kitchen. I never realized the amount of effort required to clean up the mess. Ms. Pumpkin was the head chef of the school cafeteria. And Ms. Pumpkin was the head chef in the dining hall, in the activity center. We cleaned and made ourselves useful. We had to wait for the dessert pies anyway, and it was worth the wait. All three of them smelled terrific. Even before we took them out of the oven, we could tell.

"Why don't you take the pies into the cafeteria and taste them? We can finish the cleaning in here," said Ms. Pumpkin.

And as we were eating our pies, I told them about Victor wanting to speak to Peter.

"Just before you came into the room, Ms. Pumpkin summoned Peter to the office," I said.

We discussed the possible reasons why Victor Vampire would want to have a conversation with Peter, and none of us really knew why. Pecan wanted to be reminded of how Victor looked like, so she took out her species album from her school bag. We started to look at all the different pictures of the vampires. We flipped over each page of this huge monster of a book. There were hundreds and hundreds of vampire pictures. And under each picture, there was a short description of who these creatures were. It was a short bio. As we were eating pies, we talked about the various different species.

After a while, I told them I was getting tired and might go home to rest. The morning run took all the energy right out of me, and I never really slept the night before. But just then, Primo came and sat down with us at the table. He wanted to read aloud some text language that we had to memorize from the PTLD. He was reading out some of his favorites. Then we all started to find and read out our favorites. It was actually quite fun. We even read out some of the strange ones, like MYOB. That means, "Mind your own business." Patience said her favorite one was KISS, which meant, "Keep it simple."

It was late afternoon, when Peter and Peanut arrived and sat with us. Peter told us about his conversation with Victor.

"Victor wanted to know how well I knew the president. I mean the people president. He wanted me to talk to the president about forcing Wanda to stand trial before the International Tribunal. Victor is under the impression that I can persuade the president."

We talked about what might happen with Wanda and if she was ever going to receive any type of punishment.

"Victor said the werewolves are ready to go to war with the witches if no punishment is going to be enforced," he added.

"What can we do about it?"

"There aren't very many things we can do."

We all talked about the many things ghouls have done to each other over the years. So much fighting and so many wars. We started to discuss people history and all of those wars that they have gone through. Peter provided information and insight about some of the wars, especially the recent ones and how millions and millions of people have died because of them. He started describing some of the military battles in detail. My goodness. I didn't realize Peter was such a history buff.

Pumpkin history is different from people history. It's not littered by wars, chaos, and destruction. Our history is about building, and not tearing down. To our understanding, pumpkins have never been at war with each other. Never. Ours is a peaceful history.

It seemed we had spent the whole afternoon together, just gabbing away.

And then I saw Petrina. Wow. Where was she all day?

"Where were you all day? I've been looking for you. Come on. Let's go to the lounge and catch up," I instructed.

Yes, I thought. *Finally a chance to relax and have fun.*

But Peter objected. And Petrina knew what this was about.

Lately, Peter had been trying to improve Petrina's writing skills, so he got Petrina to write something every day. It could be a poem, or short story, about any topic she was interested in. And this had to be done in a quiet place, so Peter and Petrina got up and headed toward the classrooms. Petrina asked if I wanted to come along. I thought I might as well. There were so many things I did today that I wanted to tell her. We went to a private classroom. I sat while I watched Petrina write for twenty minutes. I was going on about how I rolled down the hill, how I discovered a graphic designing website, and how I learnt three new text messages. But I don't think she listened to a word I said. She just kept writing.

It was kind of boring. It was a one-way conversation. Peter was not much of a talker. Every time I asked her to stop and come to the lounge, she would say, "Oh wait, just one more second." So I just kept talking. After a while, I stopped. Then finally, she was finished. She handed her story to Peter. We bolted for the door and went to the lounge.

Time to party. It was crowded, and we couldn't find seats. For a change, it was Petrina who said, "Oh I want to relax and sit down. Let's go to your place instead."

I wanted to stay. I actually felt like dancing. It had been quite some time since I had. I didn't dance at the Halloween party. And we missed the pumpkin New Year's Eve bash. Who else was here? I wondered if Pom Pom was here. We would have to stand regardless, so why not move around? I felt refreshed all of a sudden.

"Let's dance, Petrina!"

"Seriously. Are you psycho? No one is dancing. There's no music playing."

Just then, Polo and Plato found us. And then Pavneet and Pashelle found us.

"What did you write about today? From before?" I asked Petrina.

"I wrote that I hadn't seen my best friend Pannette all day. And then I finally met her. And I wrote down all the things that you did today. It was hard to keep up. Geez, I didn't think you could talk that fast."

"Oh. That's kind of weird."

"So when you stopped talking, after a while, I was finished too. Because I didn't have anything else to write."

"Oh," I replied. I didn't know what else to say.

"Besides. I was running out of topics to write about. You should write one too. Tomorrow."

The next day was the same as the previous day. I performed the exact same activities. First I ran with Pavneet. Then I studied math with Plato. At first it was a lot of listening and learning, but after a few sessions, I started to understand what Plato was explaining to me. Eventually, I was able to solve math equations all by myself. I drew graphs and charts. Then I would roll with Pebbles and Popeye and a whole lot of other pumpkins. Over a three-week period, I must have rolled down the hill over forty times. Then I ate lunch. This is what I did, every day, over the next three weeks. I would meet the same pumpkins, at the same time, at the exact same spot, each day. I would see Panito and Pablo cross the Water Gate Bridge at the same time as Pebbles and I crossed. We would pass by them. I would see Paxton and Pretty come out of the computer room, just as I entered. It was like everyone was following their own schedule. I would meet and talk to the same pumpkins each day at the same time. It was so weird. Each day was like déjà vu.

Pashelle and I would take turns using the computer. We each had turns using the keyboard, and we watched and learned what the other was doing. It was fun, surfing the Internet and playing games. It was exciting to learn and discover all the things we could do on a computer and on a cell phone. Porter was there to answer any questions we had.

I would study species, history, and the PTLD in the school cafeteria through the afternoons. My studying day usually ended when Petrina wrote her daily story. After a while, I started to write one too. I asked Peter one day, and he said to write about anything I wanted. I would write about all the things I had learned during the day. And then later, we would all meet up in the lounge. Sometimes we would stay, chill out, and eat dinner there. We would get something from the bar. Other times we would walk to the dining hall and eat dinner there.

My day would end saying goodnight to Peaches and Pillow.

Three days before the final exam, I passed my rolling test. I went down the hill as I usually did, with Pebbles. She had been providing one tip each day. And on that morning, when I went down the hill for that rolling lessen, Mr. Pumpkin read out my time. I rolled down the hill in forty-seven seconds. He wanted me to roll once more that morning. Popeye, who was standing next to Mr. Pumpkin, convinced me to roll again, so I walked back up the hill. This time I had noticed the amount of pumpkins on the hill, and I was the only one.

I said to myself that this was going to be my best roll ever. And it was. I knew it, even as I was rolling down.

After I had gotten up from my roll, at the bottom of the hill, I knew it was my best. As soon as my roll had ended, I sprang to my feet, and I raced over to Mr. Pumpkin. "What's my time? What's my time?" I asked.

He was surprised that I was able to rise to my feet so quickly. "Wow, Pannette. You seemed to have regained your balance right away," he said.

Well after I had rolled so many times, I didn't need as much time to regain my balance. Don't get me wrong. I was still dizzy. I was always dizzy. But this time, I got to my feet in a heartbeat. Mr. Pumpkin smiled and put his stopwatch in his pocket.

He never did tell me what my time was on that roll. Instead, he made a comment about talking to the gardener. Apparently the whole area needed resodding.

Two days before the final exam, Mr. Pumpkin came and joined us in the computer room. I showed him what I had learned on the computer and cell phone. I showed him my favorite Internet sites. We texted back and forth. I even attached pictures. I telephoned him and talked to him on the phone. I even remembered the main number for the telephone that was in the office: 1-800-PUMPKIN. He said well done. Then he said that he was shutting down the computer room for two weeks because all the computers needed upgrading.

While we were in the kitchen later that afternoon, as I watched Pecan bake another pie, I baked chocolate chip cookies. It's a simple pumpkin recipe but one that requires a lot of hard work. The cookies all had to be the same shapes and sizes. I had to ensure there were an equal number of chocolate chips in each cookie. The oven temperature had to be right. They had to stay in the oven for an exact period of time. Ms. Pumpkin was watching me. I had to pay attention to so much detail.

And when the cookies came out of the oven, she took one bite out of a cookie. She said, "Well done, Pannette. You have passed cooking class for the year!"

We all broke out in a cheer. My goodness. I just passed cooking class!

The next morning, one day before the final exam, Pavneet told me that her feet were sore. She didn't feel like running. It was strange because I did. So I ran. I ran around the school, as I had done each morning for the past three weeks. I ran around the school all by myself. When I returned back to the main door, Peter was there to greet me. He said that everyone was in the library, studying. What else. We never really did anything else on those days. We all studied for our final exam. I sat next to Peter. I stared at his face. He was so focused—so at ease. He seemed really calm. I was nervous, but I tried not to think about how nervous I was. I tried to concentrate and focus as best I could, trying not to let my mind wander off topic. I kept focus that day. When everyone was getting ready to go home, Peter wouldn't let Petrina leave or me. He asked us to write one more story. I decided to write about the experiences I had over the past three weeks.

I wrote. And I wrote. And I wrote. I only stopped writing when a security guard came into the room and asked me if I was finished yet. I guess so.

"Good. Because I was told you would be done in ten minutes, and I had to wait here all this time. I've been here for almost an hour now."

I looked around and suddenly realized that Peter and Petrina had left the room. I whispered to myself that I should go to the lounge. My friends were probably waiting for me there.

"Oh no you're not. Dr. Pumpkin needs a small favor at the hospital. I have to go home now, so you should go. You made me stay here longer than I was told, so you should do the favor," he ordered.

I didn't want to disobey him, so I said okay. I went to see Dr. Pumpkin. I saw him as soon as I walked through the hospital door.

"Hello, Pannette. What a nice surprise."

"Hello. I'm here to help. Mr. Pumpkin said you needed help."

"Oh sure. Why don't you come with me? Sit down here for one second. I was just going upstairs. But I will be right back."

He checked up on two pumpkins lying in hospital beds quickly and wrote notes on a piece of paper. Then he climbed the stairs to reach the second level. There, I could see him talk to two other doctors. I wondered what they needed help with. I got up off my chair and then looked upward again to see if the doctor was coming back down. But all three of them had left my view.

I felt like going for a walk, so I slowly walked down the main hospital aisle. I went inside a room that was occupied with a pumpkin. She was sleeping. She seemed old. I got a blanket from the closet and put it over her body, so that she would stay extra warm.

I had to disappear behind a wall when one of the nurses walked by. I didn't want to get into trouble. I didn't think I was allowed to be in that room.

I sat in the chair next to the bed. Then I started to feel sleepy. I thought about the final exam I would have a write. We have up to two hours to finish. There would be questions on all of the study material we had received throughout the school year, like math, history, species, and English.

I thought I would fail. I didn't know any of the material I was supposed to learn.

When I wasn't paying attention, the nurse came into the room. Oh no. I wasn't supposed to be here.

"I'm not doing anything, nurse," I said in my defense.

"I know. How is her temperature?"

She felt her forehead. She said, "Okay." Then she gave me a smile, and walked out the door. I guess she didn't mind that I was there that evening.

I relaxed back into the chair. I was getting tired of sitting, so I climbed into the bed and laid down next to Ms. Pumpkin.

It was so peaceful. I was thinking about what Dr. Pumpkin said to me one time. He said that a pumpkin has to be really smart and get good grades at school to be in the hospital, volunteering—that only the best and brightest volunteer their time here. I would like to be here all the time.

I had to write an exam the next morning. It was going to be ugly.

CHAPTER 13
FINAL EXAM

"Pannette. Pannette. Wake up. We have to go."

Who was it? Who was saying that? It was Peter. What was he doing in my house so early in the morning? He has been waiting outside my house each morning for the past three weeks. When I gained consciousness, I realized I was still in a hospital bed. I was lying next to Ms. Pumpkin. I must have fallen asleep. I knew why Peter was waking me up. We had to write our final exam. I was not sure that I was ready for this exercise.

I slid out of the bed. I cleaned my face. I couldn't brush my teeth, as there were no toothbrushes. After my complaint, Peter managed to find me a spare one from a closet outside the room. We left the hospital and headed toward the water gate.

We headed straight for the school, entered the classroom, and sat in our seats. I was so nervous that I didn't say anything to anyone that morning. I didn't utter a word to Peter during our walk.

I had all of my writing implements on my desk. I began to stare out into space. That's only a figure of speech, though, as none of us could see space from inside the classroom. I may have mentioned there were no windows in the room. I tried to recall some of the things I had learned, but it was no use. I was really nervous. My mind was blank. Peter noticed my anxiety and advised me to relax. We still had over twenty minutes to wait. It was a long time. Time passed slowly.

At exactly nine in the morning, Ms. Pumpkin arose from her seat and put an exam facedown on each desk. Then she sat back down and said, "You may begin."

I read the first question on the exam. It was a math question. The first few pages were all math questions. On page 5, there was a question about listing thirty text messages and their meanings, from the PTLD. But I didn't want to think about the PTLD for now. I flipped through the rest of the pages. There were history questions and species questions.

I read the first question of the exam again. I thought I knew the answer. Yes, I did. That question was easy. I hoped many of the questions would be easy.

As I was reading and answering each question, many of them were easy. As a matter of fact, most of the questions seemed basic and straightforward—not just the math questions. Some of them were very difficult, and I skipped over those ones completely. I answered the simple questions first. I recalled someone telling me to pick off the low-lying fruit from the tree first. It was an adage. It meant to do the simple tasks first, because it instills confidence. It provides a sense of accomplishment. I think that was Ms. Pumpkin.

At the end of the exam, we had to write a story. I thought about it for a minute, but I had decided to go back to the questions I had initially skipped over. I checked the time to ensure I was on a proper pace. Despite the fact that time seemed to be flying by, I was on schedule. At that point, I still had over thirty minutes remaining. I made an attempt to provide an answer to each and every question, even if I wrote anything I knew about the subject. Then I flipped back to the last few pages, where we were to write a story. I decided to write a story about my study experiences over the past three weeks. It was the exact same story I had written the previous night. Only this time, it was a much better story. A new and improved story. It seemed so much more organized and in control. I was so focused on each sentence and each paragraph. I tried to be as detailed as I could. I think it was a great story. It was a five-year-old pumpkin's account of the preparation and mental fortitude required to write an exam—the discipline, focus, and dedication that were needed. I wrote about all the effort and hard work that was necessary to learn and master all of the study material and all the time and energy that was required. I listed my accomplishments, like how I had passed the rolling, technology, and cooking classes. I wrote how much fun it could be to acquire knowledge and to experience and learn new things.

And then I was finished. I had written my exam. It took me the full two hours, and I can tell you it was the quickest two hours of my life. Time had just whizzed by. I noticed Pippa get out of her seat and hand in her exam papers to Ms. Pumpkin. I had just realized Plato had already finished and had left the room.

I waited with the rest of the students for Ms. Pumpkin to blow her whistle.

"Okay, everyone. The time is up," she said.

It would take a week for the exam results to be reported. Only at that time would I know if I passed. I hoped I did, but I doubted it. I never passed any exams. Well maybe not all of them. At least this one wasn't as difficult as the previous exams I had written during the school year. I thought I answered many of the questions correctly. I mean, some I had answered incorrectly for sure. Well, there was no sense in worrying about that now.

After the exam, we all went to the lounge. Some pumpkins were talking about this, and others that. It was idle and lazy chatter for the most part. We were all glad that school had finally ended.

Actually, over the next week, this is where many of us five-year-olds would spend our time. We all got to know each other better. There was hardly anyone else in the lounge during the daytime. All the other pumpkin students still had to write their final exam. They would do so the following week, on the same day we would receive our results. We wrote our exam one week before anyone. We were the first to finish school. Since everyone was still studying, and the elders attending to their daily duties, there was no one in the lounge except the younger pumpkins. And many elders tended to stay inside their homes, for the most part. We had the whole lounge to ourselves. Some pumpkins watched television, while others listened and danced to music. It was a party like atmosphere for a whole week, every day, all the time. It was great to just hang out.

One day, we asked Peter for more clarity on the whole Victor Vampire and the president situation.

"When did you meet the president?"

"I didn't even realize I had."

"When was this?"

"It was after the game. In the city. It was right after all that mess. You know. After dessert."

"What did he say?"

"He said something like, 'I sent a message to clean that up for you. Oh, and congratulations on that halftime award, Peter.'"

"How did he know you?"

"He must have seen my face on the big television screen."

"Wow. He has really good facial recognition. What's that ability called?"

"It's probably called facial recognition."

"So what did Victor want? Did he ask to speak with you? What did he say?"

"Yes. He wanted to speak to me. He wanted to know how close I was to the president."

"What? Are you crazy?"

"Really. That's what he wanted to know."

"Just because he shook your hand?"

"And what did you say?"

"I told him no."

"That's it?"

"Then what did he say?"

"He said that since I was speaking with the president, and sitting next to him in a box suite, at one of the biggest sporting events of the year, that I must have some influence over him. And I said I didn't know him. But it's like he doesn't believe me. He wants me to broker a meeting between him and the president. Apparently the president won't return any of his calls. Then he said he would be in touch and hung up the phone."

"Aw!" we exclaimed.

"What does that mean?"

"I don't know."

The pumpkins interrogated Peter for over an hour, asking questions about this and that. The whole situation seemed kind of weird. I mean, he actually led a plan to shed Wanda from her new power. He was one of the first to put all the facts together and make a conclusion. He set out to prove his conclusions to be correct. And he was. And now he was having secret conversations with Victor Vampire and the president? My goodness. What was the world coming to?

On the night before our exam results would be reported, we talked about the activities we all wanted to do during the summer.

Pebbles wanted to go back to the beach. Pavneet was elated she had made it to the final qualification round in golf. She thought she had a really good chance to beat Pie in the round of sixteen. She had already qualified to be on the team that would travel to Squashland. The golfers traveled there every two or three years, or something. They had a tournament against the squash. Apparently, we beat them every time. And it's no wonder. Squash are completely useless. Plato wanted to uncover the truth about how Wanda could have acquired this mystical power, which created lightning, out of thin air. He was already reading physics books to determine how it was possible to create lightning without any clouds in the sky. Polo was telling us how he, and his two brothers, Pimlico and Pony, were trying to convince the elders to allow them to travel to the city and possibly ride on some horses. Their sister Preakness was also interested. Pashelle wanted to go to the city also. She wanted to visit the Fleetwood Amusement Park. Fleetwood is a city east of New Surrey City. She and Polo were desperate to ride on the roller coaster. Plunder wanted to go also and drive in one of the bumper cars. Pluto wanted to learn dog language. Peter and Patience were finalizing a project to build an indoor swimming pool, so we could all learn how to swim. Not me. Touching the water out in Burnaby Bay was scary enough. Pecan, Pepper, and Peanut wanted the chefs to add more recipes to the food menu. They had many new ideas. Penny wanted pumpkins to learn how to use people money, so that we could buy things on our own, as opposed to using vouchers. But I was not sure what benefit that would bring to us. Petrina wanted me to help convince the elders to install windows in the classrooms. She had all kinds of suggestions to improve the school building and the study material. I was all for that. Pavneet suggested we needed air conditioning in the lounge. That was a good suggestion also. I think we needed to enlarge the lounge, so that more pumpkins could sit down.

It was getting late in the evening.

"So, Pannette. What are you doing tomorrow morning?" asked Pavneet.

"Going to school to find out how badly I failed the exam."

"I know. But what about before?"

"I don't know."

"I know. I have an idea. Let's go for a run. We haven't done that in a while."

Okay, I thought. Although it had only been two days since our last run. *But sure. Why not?* It was a nice way to spend time with Pavneet. And I wanted to run. The morning run always gave me a boost of energy. It was an accomplishment. It was an endeavor that was easy to fulfill. When I ran, I felt good about myself. We agreed to meet outside the school, at our usual spot.

The next morning, we started our run in the same manner. I was usually in the front, setting our pace. Sometimes I would run fast, then I would slow down. Sometimes I walked. And sometimes I would take a break. And she would be right next to me the whole time. That morning, we actually ran around the school two times.

We decided that we would run again during the summer. We didn't know how often, whether once or twice per week. Maybe every other day. Or maybe even every day. Who knows?

After our run, she left for her class. I entered mine and sat down in my seat. All the pumpkins were present and accounted for. Ms. Pumpkin did her usual roll call. We would receive our exam marks back soon. I would discover if I passed or failed. I hope I didn't fail. It would be the last exam of the year. I didn't want a failing mark hanging over my head all summer. I thought the worst. If I failed, then all my peers would think I was stupid, or something. It would be really embarrassing. Dr. Pumpkin would never let me volunteer at the hospital. He wouldn't think I was capable of looking after the sick and wounded pumpkins. All I needed to pass was to achieve a mark of 50 percent.

I stared at Peter. I wondered how he did. And how well Petrina did. And Pashelle. What grades would all my friends receive? Would they be happy or sad after receiving their marks? How would they feel? How would I feel if I failed? I would be so happy if I passed.

Ms. Pumpkin put my exam facedown on my desk. She normally just walked by, without looking at me. But on that day, she was sure to catch my eye before she walked further up the aisle.

I was nervous. A million thoughts were going through my head. I saw all my friends turn their exam papers over.

And after a brief hesitation and a heavy sigh, I turned over my exam paper. My hands were all sweaty. My forehead felt warm.

And the first thing I saw written was 81 percent. I got 81 percent? That was unbelievable. That meant I passed. My goodness. I passed. I was so elated. I was so relieved. All of my hard work and effort had paid off. It felt like a huge weight had been lifted off my shoulders.

I looked around the room to see the faces of the other pumpkins. They were all looking down at their exams. They were flipping through the pages and reading the notes from the elders. They were reading the correct answers to the questions they had gotten wrong, no doubt.

The only pumpkin who wasn't looking down was Ms. Pumpkin. She had watched me turn over my exam paper. She was staring right at me, with her shining and glistening eyes. She seemed so happy for me. She seemed just as elated as I was. I think it was the first time I had seen her smile at me all year. I couldn't help but return the smile. I mean, I was ecstatic. I had just received a mark of 81 percent!

She said something to me as she was staring right into my eyes. She whispered something. It was hard to make out what she said. I had to watch her lips move.

She said, "Good job!"

To Lindy.

Peter Nanra

CPSIA information can be obtained
at www.ICGtesting.com
Printed in the USA
LVOW13s1228260117
522202LV00011B/69/P